Hurrah! Maxie Pichelsteiner, the tiny, two-inch-tall man, and the characters from the first book, *The Little Man*, are back with further adventures.

Having fulfilled his dream of becoming a circus performer with his friend and now his partner, Professor Hokus von Pokus, Maxie finds himself swept up into the whirl of movie-making about the life of none other than the Little Man himself! Adventures by the dozen fill this second volume.

Artist Stanley Mack's illustrations capture the world of the Little Man. And, once again, Erich Kästner's charming fantasy, translated from the German, will enchant readers with its wryly humorous style and imaginative themes.

THE LITTLE MAN AND THE BIG THIEF

ERICH KÄSTNER

THE LITTLE MAN AND THE BIG THIEF

TRANSLATED BY JAMES KIRKUP

PICTURES BY

STANLEY MACK

Alfred A. Knopf / New York

THE LITTLE MAN
AND THE BIG THIEF

INTRODUCTION

These were the two tiniest members of the Chinese acrobat troupe "The Bamboo Family" of Stilke's Circus, twenty inches tall. But actually they come from Pichelstein in the forests of Bohemia and aren't Chinese at all. The Bohemian town of Pichelstein is famous for two reasons: all the inhabitants are of very small stature, and they are all outstanding gymnasts and acrobats.

This is their son. He is called Maxie Pichelsteiner, alias the Little Man; as he measures only two inches, he sleeps in a matchbox. At the age of six he lost his parents.

This is Professor Hokus von Pokus, the circus magician. He is taking care of the Little Man, bringing him up and teaching him reading, writing, and arithmetic.

This is Winsome Waldemar, a tailor's dummy until he was bought by Hokus. Why? Because Maxie, tiny as he was, wanted to become an artiste. He had to scramble and climb for months all over Winsome Waldemar until he had mastered all the tricks necessary for the performance of a sensational circus act.

This is Maxie's house, drawn to scale; it was a gift from King Bileam of Breganzona.

Here is Rosa Marzipan. Rosa is a pretty trampoline acrobat in the circus and good friend of Maxie and Professor Hokus von Pokus.

Here are Bernhard and Bald Otto, members of an international gangster's band, who once kidnapped Maxie.

6

This is Jakob Hurtig, the boy who rescued Maxie from the kidnappers.

Now I'll tell you in as few words as possible what happened after the arrest of Bernhard and Bald Otto. They were taken to the police station for interrogation, and each sat in his own cell, safely separated from the other. Bernhard just stared sulkily at the bare wall. But Bald Otto pounded the cell door with his fists. "I want my bottle of brandy back!" he yelled. "You nabbed it from under my very nose! That's contrary to all human rights!"

Then the spyhole in the cell door opened, and a warden asked in an unfriendly manner, "What do you want back?" "My bottle of brandy!" screamed Bald Otto. "You must be out of your mind," snarled the warden. "From now on, it's clink, not drink!"

The next morning the two prisoners were escorted under strong guard to the police court. Detective Inspector Steinbeiss wanted to interrogate them with Maxie present, for the Little Man was not only the victim of but also the chief witness to their crime. Hokus von Pokus put Maxie in his breast pocket, and off they went. Jakob Hurtig was also asked to come forward as a witness, and he was driven from school in a police car. His classmates were green with envy. Especially as they were sweating over mental arithmetic.

So Maxie, Hokus, and Jakob met up once again with Herr Steinbeiss, and this is the beginning of . . .

1

Detective Inspector Steinbeiss, whose name means "Stonebite,"
actually bites on stone—granite to be exact · Bernard has a complex,
and Bald Otto has a big thirst · A tourist party from Paris lands
at Tempelhof Airport · Mr. John Drinkwater, six and a half feet
tall and in a hurry, arrives from Hollywood

"What we know up to the present about the two rogues is hardly worth mentioning," said Detective Inspector Steinbeiss. "We have their passports, their plane tickets, and their fingerprints. The passports are forgeries. The plane tickets are for Madrid, but I don't believe they would have stayed there long."

"But fingerprints can't be forged," Maxie said. He was sitting in the middle of the desk on the rim of the ashtray, swinging his legs. "Fingerprints are always genuine."

"They're extraordinarily accurate!" agreed Jakob Hurtig. "Every human being has his own. Not even twins have the same fingerprints. And anyone who has already been in

9

prison is done for. The police match the new fingerprints with the previous ones, and it's all up with the crook."

"Do you suppose we've been napping?" the Inspector asked. "We haven't had a wink of sleep." He yawned jaw-splittingly. "Interpol in Paris, Scotland Yard in London, the F.B.I. in Washington, and the Federal Criminal Investigation Bureau in Wiesbaden were all immediately notified."

Professor Hokus von Pokus was surprised. "Why beat about the bush? The two villains kidnapped Maxie and intended to smuggle him out of the country. For that they should go to prison, and their conviction is certain. What their real names may be and whether they previously stole gold watches has nothing to do with the matter!"

"Not for you. But it has for us," Inspector Steinbeiss patiently explained. "In the first place, if they have criminal records, their next sentences will be heavier. And in the second place, we would really like to get the elusive Señor Lopez under lock and key. Bald Otto told The Little Man lots of interesting things. Perhaps I too can persuade him to talk a little."

"Are you going to torture him?" asked Maxie.

"Don't be silly," growled Inspector Steinbeiss.

"For a thief, he was really quite decent to me. He's more stupid than wicked."

"The stupid ones are also dangerous," stated the Inspector.

At that moment Maxie toppled over and fell into the ashtray. When he had hauled himself upright again, he didn't look very clean, and he sneezed.

Hokus fished the little fellow out of the cigar ash, dusted him down as well as possible, and told him, "Ashtrays are no place for nonsmokers. Take note of that!"

In the waiting room outside the Inspector's office stood two brown wooden benches. On one of the benches, between two uniformed police sergeants, sat Bald Otto. And on the other bench sat Bernhard, also between two police sergeants.

"All this confounded waiting around," grumbled Bald Otto. "You have to hang around like at the dentist's."

Bernhard gazed at him threateningly. "But at the dentist's you have to open your mouth wide. With the police, on the other hand . . ."

"No talking!" one of the sergeants cried angrily.

"Keep your traps shut!" commanded another.

"You hear that?" Bernhard asked, and laughed craftily. "Even the police want you to stop your jawing."

"That goes for you, too!" shouted the third sergeant furiously. "Not another word!"

"Okay," Bernhard replied.

"Okay," repeated Bald Otto and looked across at Bernhard in a worried way. Then all six men were silent while they waited.

Bernhard was summoned first. He sat down opposite the Inspector, crossed his legs, and cast a fleeting glance at the others in the room. He did not pay any special attention to The Little Man, who was now squatting on an open cigarette box. He gazed nonchalantly around the ugly office and drawled, "Nice place you have here."

Jakob Hurtig giggled, but the Inspector was in no mood for jokes. He was too tired. "Less of the funny stuff! You and your accomplice abducted the minor, Maxie Pichelsteiner, circus artiste, from a Berlin hotel, kept him prisoner in an empty house and planned to fly abroad with him."

"Before you go any further, I'd like to get one point straight," Bernhard said. "I alone, dressed as a waiter and without Otto's assistance, abducted this minor, Maxie Pichelsteiner, circus artiste. And that we intended to take him abroad with us is an unproven and unprovable assertion on your part."

"So you did not intend abducting him to South America?"

"I should think not! What? That squeaky little monster?"
Bernhard shuddered with horror. "To South America? What
for? All I know of that place is in my school atlas."

Maxie jumped up and threatened him with his fists.
"You're lying! You were going to take me to Señor Lopez!"

"Lopez?" asked Bernhard. "Never heard of him."

"Very well. And why did you steal The Little Man in the
first place?" the Inspector asked.

"That's a long story."

"Make it short," the Inspector told him.

"You see, I have this complex," Bernhard began. "And
even as a child I had this complex, see? Whenever I saw an
empty matchbox, I picked it up, put some little beastie in it,
and carried it around with me. Sometimes it was a ladybird
or a bumblebee or a butterfly. Or a black beetle. Or a blue-
bottle. Then it would buzz and hum and flutter about in the
box. And when I read about The Little Man in the news-
paper and the matchbox he slept in, well, I just couldn't
resist."

"But I'm not a beetle!" Maxie cried angrily.

"These complexes," sighed Bernhard.

The Inspector pressed a button. "Very pleased to hear about your complex, I'm sure, Herr . . . Herr . . . What *is* your name by the way? Or better still, what *was* your name when you used to hunt for bumblebees in the bushes?"

"I should very much like to be of assistance to you," said Bernhard, "but I've completely forgotten my name and the date and place of my birth. It was all so long ago."

A police sergeant entered the office.

"Take him away!" ordered Inspector Steinbeiss. "And bring the other one in."

Now it was Bald Otto sitting in the chair that Bernhard had been sitting in. He gazed vacantly at the top of the desk.

"Hello!" cried Maxie.

"I don't speak to the likes of you," said Otto. "I was like a mother to you, but you turned me in. Stomach-ache and valerian drops it was, and like a booby I went out to get the drops—oh, it's enough to make any man lose his faith in human beings." He shook his bald head perplexedly. "What's going to become of the world if lads as little as him get that discheatful!"

"Deceitful," Jakob Hurtig corrected him.

Otto flapped his hand wearily. "It's the same difference, mate. Like chalk and cheese. I'm a good soul, I am, generous to a fault, I am, but he squealed on me. It's not what you expect of a midget. Stool pigeon!"

14

"It seems to me that for a kidnapper you've got a bit too high an opinion of yourself," Hokus remarked drily, bending forward.

"I'm never going to open my mouth again," declared Otto, " 'cept for the dentist."

"That would be unwise of you," said the Inspector. Then from his side drawer he produced a bottle of brandy and a glass, placed them both on the desk, and smiled invitingly, as if he were Otto's favorite uncle. "*You* didn't steal The Little Man. Your accomplice, Bernhard, pulled that job. All the same, you made yourself an accessory to the act. That too is a serious crime. But 'accessory' is an elastic term."

Bald Otto stared as if hypnotized at the full bottle and the empty glass.

"It is for the law to decide what degree of punishment shall be meted out to you." Inspector Steinbeiss half filled the glass, shoved it across to Otto, and said, "Cheers!"

Otto seized the glass, and before the others could say Jack Robinson, it was empty. He gave a grunt of blissful satisfaction, put the glass back on the desk, took a deep breath, and asked, "Well, whaddya wanta know?"

"While you were holding The Little Man prisoner, you told him about a certain Señor Lopez. You said that he is the richest man in the world and that he lives in a secret fortress somewhere between Santiago and Valparaiso, collects Old Masters and young ballerinas, and is protected by armed guards—a hundred crack shots. You said that you and Bernhard abducted a gipsy woman from Lisbon two years ago and that she has to tell Lopez' fortune by the cards every day. What more do you know about this man and his accomplices? Did he give you direct orders to kidnap The Little Man? When and where? Or was there a middleman? If so, who?"

Otto stared hard at the bottle, ran his tongue over his lips, and remained silent.

"You scratch my back, and I'll scratch yours," said the Inspector. "You help me, and I'll help you." He refilled the glass halfway. "Cheers!"

This time Bald Otto took his time. He drank in tiny sips, gave himself a good shake as if to distribute the brandy evenly inside him, and then said, "That's the biggest cock-and-bull story I've heard in all my born days! It's enough to make your eyes pop right out of your head!"

The others gazed at him flabbergasted. Maxie waved his arms wildly and shrieked angrily, "I'm not lying!"

"Of course not," said Otto. "Lying is too good a word to describe that kind of story. It's a world record, my lad. So much imagination in such a little head—how d'you do it?"

"I'm not lying!" screamed Maxie piercingly. "That's a mean dirty thing to say!"

Professor Hokus von Pokus tugged nervously at his elegant beard. "I'm a peaceable sort of man," he said, "but now my fists are beginning to itch." He slowly stood up.

"Bravo!" cried Jakob Hurtig. "Bash the living daylights out of him!" His cheeks had gone bright red.

Then the Inspector pounded the desk with his fist so energetically that Maxie involuntarily jumped into the air. "Take it easy," Inspector Steinbeiss growled. He put the bottle back in his drawer and pressed the bell. "One last question for the time being," he said grimly to Bald Otto. "If there's no Señor Lopez, why should a drunken Goldilocks, I mean Moldilocks, I mean Baldylocks like you have kidnapped the boy at all?"

Otto's eyes became round. "You don't know what you're saying. First you tell me fair and square that it wasn't me that done it, but Bernhard. And now all of a sudden I'm expected to know why I done it. I was only an accessory, and that's an awfully elastic term. You better ask Bernhard!"

A sergeant came into the room. "Take him away!" roared the Inspector.

As soon as Otto left the room, Steinbeiss staggered across to the sofa in the corner, sat down, pulled off his boots, and said, "It's only afternoon now, but I haven't had a wink of sleep for twenty-four hours. Good night." Then he flopped back. The sofa springs squealed like a score of piglets at feeding time. Steinbeiss was dead to the world.

The next afternoon two things happened that concern our story.

First, Mr. Drinkwater arrived in Berlin.

Second, at Orly, the great airport in Paris, Operation Sleeping Beauty was launched, though this strange name was not given to the "operation" until it was too late. People are always smarter after the event. After the event it was discovered that a chartered plane with thirty-eight passengers aboard had taken off at four o'clock in the afternoon from Orly Airport for Berlin. Such tourist flights are nothing unusual; nor was it in any way remarkable that the tourist group should be composed entirely of men. Perhaps they belonged to a bowling team or a football team.

The flight to Berlin went off smoothly. The plane was parked in a hanger. It had been chartered for three days, and the return flight had been paid for in advance. The leader of the tour, a Monsieur Boileau, asked the pilot of the plane to give him the telephone number of his hotel because he might be flying back to Paris with his group earlier than expected. With that he took his leave and went to join his clients, who were already standing beside the conveyor belt in the arrival hall, waiting for their luggage. If you had seen them hoisting their heavy bags onto their shoulders, you would certainly not have taken them for members of a bowling team or a male voice choir. But unfortunately you were not at the airport. Ah, well, one can't be everywhere at once.

That same afternoon, as I have already mentioned, Mr. Drinkwater also arrived in Berlin. John Foster Drinkwater, one of the great American film producers. He was certainly a great man: six and a half feet tall in his socks.

Originally he had intended to send his company's European representative, because it was thanks to him that he had had the first reports of the sensational events involving

The Little Man. But then Mr. Drinkwater in person, making the most of all his inches, had zoomed into action. Hollywood–New York–London–Berlin—the cities flew by. He *had* to film Maxie, cost what it may. He only hoped that his business rivals had not already got wind of the colossal opportunity just waiting to be exploited. It was now or never!

When he arrived at the Hilton Hotel in Budapest Street and unfolded his great length out of the taxi, the manager of the hotel and all his staff were in attendance, bowing and scraping before him at the entrance.

Because they were bowing so low, he quipped, "What's lost?" Before they had time to titter politely at this witticism, he was already at the elevator. And before they got to the elevator, he was already in his room and on the telephone. And here begins . . .

Brausewetter, the ringmaster of the circus, changes the color of his gloves · Rosa Marzipan lends Mr. Drinkwater a pair of opera glasses · Film negotiations in the Blue Salon · Some people are not allowed to sleep at night, others cannot sleep at night, and yet others will not sleep at night

Mr. Drinkwater was indefatigable. "I sleep only twice a year," he used to say, "in July and in December. But then I sleep right through both months, day after day, twenty-four hours a day, without waking."

When people expressed amazement and asked whether he at least got up from time to time to partake of a snack, he would reply, "No. I don't do things by halves. I spend my two sleeping months on my yacht *Sleepwell*. Besides the captain and crew, I have two reliable employees on board. One of them has to eat for me, and the other has to wash for me." It was impossible to tell whether he was kidding or not, for he kept a perfectly straight face.

Once in Berlin, John Foster Drinkwater, the long drink of water and movie mogul from the U.S.A., was no slouch. He telephoned Hokus von Pokus. He telephoned the ringmaster of the circus, Brausewetter. He telephoned Inspector Steinbeiss, who was not exactly happy about the call because he was still sleeping on the sofa. He telephoned the American Consul-General. He telephoned the Bank of Germany. And he telephoned the Frankfurt branch of his film company. Then he took a shower. For himself, as it was neither July nor December.

Later he dined in the hotel's Golden City Bar; he had a stew covered with toasted cheese, made especially for him. And at the beginning of the circus performance he was sitting in a specially reserved box. Ringmaster Brausewetter greeted him effusively, wearing snow-white kid gloves. He asked whether he might introduce his celebrated guest to the packed, excited house.

"Why ask me?" retorted Drinkwater. "Why don't you ask him?"

Brausewetter clapped his white kid gloves to his head. "You don't understand!" he cried worriedly. "It is *you* who are the celebrated guest."

"Now look here!" Drinkwater retorted angrily. "I came here as a businessman. Too much advance publicity sends up prices. Will you do me a favor?"

"Of course."

"Then kindly keep your smart white gloves over that mouth of yours until our contract is signed."

"I trust you mean that only in a metaphorical sense," Brausewetter replied sharply. "I'll be going."

Mr. Drinkwater riffled through the program and said nonchalantly, "I thought you'd already left."

In the Professor's dressing room the ringmaster, deeply offended, related what had just happened. "What a rude way to talk!" he stormed. "Telling me to keep my mouth shut!"

"It was not very polite," Hokus agreed. "But, of course, he's right. He doesn't want his competitors to get wind of the deal and offer us more money than he does."

"What's that got to do with us?" The ringmaster twirled his moustache up at the ends. "We should come to an agreement with the one who makes the biggest offer."

Hokus smilingly shook his head. "We shall come to an agreement with the best man, and that is Mr. Drinkwater. Allow me to refresh your memory, my dear Brausewetter. Some time ago, not so very long ago either, the number called 'The Big Thief and The Little Man' was a sensational success in the circus world. The fees that were offered the two artistes by your competitors were colossal. Did I run where the money was?"

Brausewetter, pained, gazed down at the toes of his black kid pumps. "No, but the new contract you signed with me wasn't peanuts either."

"I expected you to bring that up," said Hokus. "My motto is: the best possible contract with the best possible man. That goes for you, and it goes for Mr. Drinkwater. Now have we got that straight?"

"Right you are, Herr Professor!" Brausewetter clicked his heels, turned about, and marched to the door. There he collided with blond Rosa Marzipan.

She was wearing tights and a tutu, because she was on her way to the ring, where she would perform aerial acrobatics on the trampoline with her two sisters.

"Is it all settled?" she cried. "Shall I keep our movie mogul company during the interval?" "You better watch out," Brausewetter warned her. "Our movie mogul has sharp teeth. He bites."

"Not me," declared Rosa, spinning round in a pirouette.

"Go and sit nicely in his box, darling," Hokus told her.

She dropped a deep curtsy and darted down the alley leading to the ring.

The performance went, as any performance should, according to plan. The artistes, the clowns, the horses, and even the tigers seemed to be making a special effort. The audience too was in top form. And even Mr. Drinkwater was enjoying himself. He frequently jotted down notes. It looked as if he were awarding marks. He was probably adding up sums. It's a way businessmen have. They even add up in their dreams.

During the long intermission most people left their seats, but he remained where he was. When Rosa Marzipan, now wearing a silvery dress, came along, he stood up. "You were very good," he remarked. "And you are very pretty."

Smiling with amusement, she gave him her hand. "It's good to have one's true worth appreciated," she said. After they had sat down, she took a pair of opera glasses out of her evening bag and held them out to him.

He took them, playfully gazed at Rosa through them, and nodded. "Quite extraordinarily pretty!"

"I can see you're a ladies' man, Mr. Drinkwater," she remarked drily. "But you need look through them only when Hokus and Maxie come on!"

"Pity," he said.

The second half of the program turned out to be even more brilliant than the first. And no wonder. Everyone was waiting in a fever of excitement for the great sensation, the number called "The Big Thief and The Little Man." And when Professor Hokus von Pokus entered the ring to thunderous applause, Mr. Drinkwater clamped Rosa Marzipan's opera glasses firmly to his eyes. He took them away only after Emma, the white dove, had returned from her flight round the big top with Maxie on her back and had delivered her passenger safely into the Professor's hand.

For twenty-eight minutes he had been not the celebrated film producer Drinkwater but merely one of several thousand enchanted spectators. He had laughed with them. He had been astounded, as they were. He had shared their suspense. He had clapped as they did.

And when the circular grille rose up out of the floor, he, like all the others, dashed into the ring in order to get a final look at The Little Man waving to them all through the bars. For despite his opera glasses, Mr. Drinkwater had not clapped eyes on him for so much as an instant.

Miss Marzipan had kept her eye on the gentleman from

Hollywood all the time. Nothing had escaped her. Now she realized that he was not just a cold-hearted businessman who saw numbers instead of life, employees rather than human beings, and the price tag on a bunch of flowers rather than the flowers themselves.

But when he had shoved his way back through the excited crowds to his box, he became once more the cold-hearted calculating machine. "It'll be difficult to light the big top," he said with annoyance. "But I must get that flight on the dove into the can, as sharp and clear as through a magnifying glass. Don't you have any solid structures in your country? Circuses made of stone? With firmly fixed platforms for the floodlights in the roof? And for my cameramen? If not, the insurance rates for photography in a four-post big top are going to be fantastically high."

Rosa became practical. In Munich, she told him, there was the Krone Circus building. Right on the City Square. Not far from the main railway station. A solid structure, renovated only a few years ago.

"Can it be rented?" asked Drinkwater.

"Why bother?" Miss Marzipan replied. "We play there from time to time. We're booked there this year."

I hope not in December, for then I'll be sleeping."

"Herr Brausewetter has booked us there for October and November," said Rosa.

"Okay," said Drinkwater. "Munich'll be fine. And two months—that's good. We'll shoot the circus in the circus and the studio scenes at the Bavaria in Grünwald. Pichelstein is not very far away, is it?"

"What on earth are you going to do in Pichelstein?"

"That's where our film will begin!" he explained. "In the little village with the little houses and the little inhabitants who are gymnasts. And we'll have Maxie's little parents walking to the little station with their little bags, on their way to seek their fortune in the great wide world. Or can you think of a better opening?"

Laughing, she shook her head. "It's the best there is, Mr. Drinkwater."

"Call me John," he said, flattered.

The people sitting near them were growing restless. They were all hissing and shushing. One of them even said, "For goodness' sake, hold your tongues!"

After the performance they all met in the Blue Salon of the hotel where Hokus and Maxie were staying. There were five persons present: Rosa Marzipan, John F. Drinkwater, The Little Man, Hokus von Pokus and, ill at ease in a corner, the ringmaster, Brausewetter. He was wearing dark gray gloves. Half mourning, so to speak. His moustache, slicked with pomade, was at half mast. Perhaps the movie mogul from Hollywood was still angry with him.

"Look!" whispered Maxie, fascinated, when Mr. Drinkwater made his appearance. "He just goes up and up and up! Just the thing for me! A live climbing-pole!"

"Behave yourself!" Hokus said sternly. The Little Man sat on the table and sipped a spoonful of hot chocolate.

"Aye, aye, cap'n," Maxie whispered.

Drinkwater lit a huge black cigar and then declared, "I want to film Maxie Pichelsteiner's life story, and naturally he must play the part himself. I intend to give the other chief parts not to actors but to yourselves. Good artistes are almost always reliable actors."

"And who'll play the ringmaster of the circus?" asked Brausewetter cautiously.

Drinkwater grinned. "You, of course. Or perhaps you know of someone better? No? Me neither."

Brausewetter's wilting moustache perked up again. Then, under cover of the table, he stealthily took off his dark gray gloves and put them away. A few seconds later he was wearing snow-white gloves! It was not magic. He always carried a white pair, a gray pair, and a black pair with him, and he changed them according to his mood of the moment. He couldn't get through the day without them.

Mr. Drinkwater described in detail how he envisaged the film, including when and where he wanted to film it. He himself would direct it. He suggested the names of two actors to play the parts of the two kidnappers, because, he quipped, the real rascals, Bernhard and Bald Otto, were most unlikely to obtain leave from the prison authorities to make the film. So far, he felt, all was clear. "There's only one thing lacking," he declared. "Something very important. A love story. You've got to have a love interest in every movie. But I'll think of one."

At that Maxie laughed out loud and almost choked himself on the hot chocolate.

"Perhaps we could help you," said Rosa Marzipan, with a straight face. "How would it be if in your film one of the three trampoline artistes fell in love with the conjurer? And the conjurer fell in love with the pretty blonde trampoline artiste?"

Drinkwater drew on his Havana and considered it. "Not a bad idea. But the dramatic conflict is still missing from it. That's the most important. That's what the public wants. A happy ending without a struggle of some kind doesn't go down well in a movie."

"That might be provided too," said Brausewetter, daintily stroking his white kid-gloved left hand with his right. "If, for example, one of the clowns were jealous of the conjurer and in the dressing room secretly exchanged the latter's tailcoat for the haute école rider's . . ."

"You've got me on the edge of my seat already," said Drinkwater excitedly.

"And what if the haute école rider wearing the conjurer's tailcoat rides into the ring without suspecting that the exchange has been made. And what if suddenly huge bunches of paper flowers burst out of this wrong tailcoat, and two tame white doves fly out, and the white rabbit hops out into the ring, and the stallion takes fright, rears, and throws the famous haute école rider into the sawdust?"

"Wonderful!" cried Mr. Drinkwater. "That'll do the trick! Love, jealousy, suspense, mistaken tailcoats, comedy

28

sequence in front of a packed house, the haute école rider whips the clown, the conjurer kisses the trampoline artiste— who could ask for anything more? The only question is whether a gentleman as distinguished as Professor Hokus von Pokus would consent to play the part of a lover." He glanced across at the "distinguished gentleman" and his eyes popped with amazement.

For Miss Marzipan, the professional trampoline artiste, had wound her arms tenderly round the conjurer and said, "You bet he'll consent."

And Hokus, a bit embarrassed, added, "Looks as if I'll have to."

"Aha," said Mr. Drinkwater. "I'm beginning to see the light. Real life has forestalled me."

"That's right," said Brausewetter, still in a white-glove mood. "The clown and the switched tailcoats and the fall from the horse—everything happened just like that a few weeks ago in my circus!"

"Three cheers for real life!" cried Mr. Drinkwater, looking pleased. "Sometimes life itself gets ideas as good as those dreamed up by film people." The others all laughed at this, and he laughed as heartily as the rest.

But then he suddenly became dead serious; he sat up straight as a ramrod and said, "Well, that's enough about what may be called 'artistic' matters for the present. Sure, it's important. But now we must begin the most important aspect of our conference—the business side of things."

"I suggest a postponement," said Hokus. "Our little chap

must be off to bed. It's high time."

"Put him to bed in his matchbox," the American suggested. "Then we can go on with our business."

Hokus shook his head vigorously. "Out of the question. He's my partner." Then suddenly he gave a start. "Where is he, anyway?"

It was as if a thunderbolt had fallen. They all gaped at the table. The Little Man had vanished!

"Maxie!" cried Hokus.

"Where are you, pet?" called Rosa Marzipan.

"Come on, son!" shouted Brausewetter.

No response.

"Maxie!" yelled Mr. Drinkwater.

They sat there as still as statues and held their breath. Nothing. Not a sound. But outside the door someone could be heard walking up and down.

With one bound Hokus was at the door. He tore it open.

"Who's there?" he shouted.

"Now, Herr Professor," the man outside answered, "you know who I am. I'm the hotel detective detailed to guard Maxie."

"And where is he?"

"What do you mean?" asked the detective, puzzled. "He's with you. I've been watching your door all this time to see that he's not kidnapped again."

"He's gone!" shrieked Brausewetter, hastily tugging off his white kid gloves.

"That's quite impossible," said the detective. "The Blue

Salon has only this one door, and ever since you went in I have never taken my eyes off it."

"Then why doesn't he answer when we call him?" Mr. Drinkwater asked nervously. "He's disappeared!"

"Out of the question." The detective was not to be flustered. "Your tie has disappeared too, but it must still be here somewhere."

So it had! Drinkwater's gaudy tie had vanished.

"Start looking!" Rosa Marzipan said cheerfully. "Gentlemen, down on your knees!"

And the men crawled around the Blue Salon on their hands and knees.

It's a pity there was no one there to photograph them. It would have made a marvelous candid camera shot.

Rosa did not crawl on the floor. Her skirt was too tight, and she thought it was enough to have four men at her feet.

So she searched the upper regions: the little corner tables, the sideboards, the bookshelves, the glass-fronted cabinet with its pieces of antique porcelain, and the charming old Victorian writing desk. One of the desk drawers was open, and over the edge dangled the end of a brightly colored tie made of soft foulard silk.

Rosa carefully lifted the end of the tie and said excitedly, "Here he is, the little rascal!" The men were on their feet in a trice. They rushed to the desk, dusting their knees, and gazed thankfully into the open drawer. Maxie was asleep. Sound as a doormouse. He did not wake up when Hokus lifted him and laid him carefully in the hollow of his hand. He left the Blue Salon walking on tiptoe.

Only when they reached their bedroom upstairs and Hokus had placed Maxie in the old matchbox did The Little Man open his eyes for an instant, murmuring, "I was so tired." Then he went straight off to sleep again.

The hotel detective sat down on a chair in the corridor outside the bedroom, drank hot coffee and kept watch. He was not allowed to sleep.

Mr. Drinkwater drove back to the Hilton and began calculating. For he couldn't sleep.

And somewhere in the big city sat Monsieur Boileau and his group of strange tourists from Paris. *They* didn't want to go to sleep. They had sinister plans to discuss. Plans for the following day.

And on the next day, though not with the strange tourist group, begins . . .

· 3 ·

*Talking of business matters · Arithmetic is also a part of life ·
The mysterious envelope · Herr von Goethe as a teacher of business
methods · The second sealed envelope · Negotiations
successfully concluded*

The business negotiations began immediately after breakfast.
A hotel detective was again guarding the Blue Salon, but it
was a different man. The detective who had kept watch the
previous evening and all through the night was naturally
tired and had to sleep. The two detectives relieved each other
every twelve hours.

Since I cannot skip the conference in the Blue Salon, I shall
give only the barest outline of the business negotiations.

"Well, I've put to you what I want to buy and why,"
began Mr. Drinkwater. "Now it's your turn, Professor.
Name your price."

"First show him the envelope," Maxie advised. He was
once more sitting at his little table on the big table and eating
a pineapple tart with a tiny spoon.

"What envelope?" Drinkwater asked, puzzled.

Rosa Marzipan smiled impishly. "We circus folk are an
artful lot, my dear John."

"Our price is written on a slip of paper," explained Maxie. "The slip of paper is in an envelope. The envelope is sealed. And the sealed envelope is in the inside pocket of my agent and partner, Hokus von Pokus."

Brausewetter, the ringmaster, was startled and hurt. "It's the first I've heard about it!" he complained. He tugged off his gray gloves and, contrary to his usual custom, sat for about half an hour with bare hands because he did not know whether he would have to put on his white or his black gloves.

"My dear Brausewetter," said Hokus, "the contract between your circus and Mr. Drinkwater is your own affair. We have nothing to do with that. On the slip of paper in the envelope is written simply the price that Maxie, Miss Marzipan, and I desire."

"Your sealed envelope makes me nervous," admitted Mr. Drinkwater. "I want to make a wide-screen Technicolor movie. In addition, I intend to produce the story of Maxie's life in six episodes for the TV market. All that'll cost a pretty penny, so I need the world rights for ten years. And therefore I need your Maxie, yourself, and your good lady as starring performers for the months of October and November at the Krone Circus in Munich. I hope that's now crystal clear."

"But," replied Hokus, "never before was there a movie star only two inches tall. The world has never seen anything like it before, so everyone in the whole world will rush off to see your movie at the nearest theater."

34

"And you'll be rolling in money!" cried Maxie excitedly. The others gazed at him disapprovingly.

"All right," Drinkwater said. "Let's say our film may really do big business. But what's all this about a sealed envelope? And where is it?"

Hokus took an envelope out of his inside breast pocket, laid it on the table and said, "Here you are." But when the American put out his hand to take it, Hokus stopped him. "The envelope will be opened only after you have written on another slip of paper the sum of money you are willing to pay us."

"Roundabout way of doing business, isn't it?" Drinkwater growled. "Then I suppose we open your silly little envelope, compare the two figures, and begin to bargain. So why all this melodrama with the envelopes?"

"Just a minute!" cried Maxie. "The best part is still to come." And he rubbed his little hands with glee.

"We shall not bargain with one another," Hokus explained. "The sums written on both slips of paper are decisive. If your figure is higher than ours, then the deal is on."

"And what if I offer a lesser figure than the one inside your envelope?"

"Then," replied Rosa, smiling sweetly, "the deal is off."

At that, Mr. Drinkwater did something he rarely did—he looked flabbergasted. He was silent.

And Brausewetter put on one black glove and one white one. He was thus prepared for anything.

After a pause Mr. Drinkwater lit one of his black cigars, stared at the cloud of smoke he produced, gazed worriedly at the mysterious envelope, and said, "It's a new method of doing business. You're very smart."

"You're wrong on both points," retorted Hokus. "We don't understand anything about business matters. And the method is almost a hundred and fifty years old."

"It was invented by Goethe!" cried Maxie. "The great German poet."

"Never heard of him," snapped Drinkwater. "And this Goethe discovered the trick with the envelope, did he? But there were no film producers in those days!"

Rosa laughed. "But there were book publishers all right, and they were just as bad."

"Businessmen are in this world to do business," snapped Drinkwater. "What's to become of us if poets and conjurers start putting sealed envelopes on the negotiating table?"

"It actually happened," remarked Hokus. "One publisher, I think he was called Göschen, wanted to publish Goethe's next book and inquired what the manuscript would cost. The great poet sent a good friend to see the publisher and presented him with the envelope. If the publisher proposed less than what was demanded in the envelope, the affair was to be considered . . ."

"No deal!" cried Maxie gleefully.

"And how was the matter settled?" Drinkwater asked.

"The publisher thought about it rather a long time."

"I can well believe it," said the American. He mopped his

forehead with his handkerchief. He was feeling hot round the collar, too. "And then?"

"Then he quoted a very high figure. It was the highest he could manage. Then the envelope was opened and the two figures were compared. The publisher's offer was higher than what Goethe had demanded, so the deal was made."

"Your great Goethe was a great cutthroat," Drinkwater declared grimly. "Pity you read his account books as well as his poetry."

"We don't want to press you," Hokus replied calmly. "You can always turn down our offer."

"No, that I cannot do. I must and will make the film about The Little Man. And so I must buy the world rights."

"All right," said Hokus. "Then we'll expect an offer from you. If your figure is more than the one in our envelope, everything will be fine. Think it over quietly. There's no hurry."

"I don't need to think it over," growled Drinkwater. "I know the biggest figure I can give you without going bankrupt." He got up, strode across to the desk, rapidly wrote something on a slip of paper, came back, shoved the paper over to Hokus, said "There!" and fell back into his chair.

Hokus read the figure and was silent. Rosa glanced at the paper and said "Oh!"

Brausewetter looked over Hokus's shoulder and muttered, "Ye gods and little fishes!"

And Maxie, who had run to the edge of the slip of paper in order to read the figure, jumped on Hokus from the table

top, scrambled up him like a squirrel, gave him a kiss on the tip of the nose and, after an elegant slalom, finished up in his partner's cosy breast pocket.

"Congratulations," said Professor Hokus von Pokus solemnly. "You have won."

Mr. Drinkwater heaved a sigh of relief.

"We'll take great pains to make the shooting a success," cried Maxie. "And when the film's in the can, we can take it easy."

Brausewetter's moustache seemed to shrink with shock. "You're not going to leave me and my circus in the lurch?"

"No," said Hokus, "but we'll certainly take two months' holiday."

38

Now you probably want to know what was written on Mr. Drinkwater's paper. Well, this is what was on the slip of paper:

Two million dollars! It's not every day one earns such a pile of money. Certainly not conjurers and Little Men. Not to mention trampoline artistes.

"Now I know the film rights belong to me," said Mr. Drinkwater. "And what I have to pay for them, unfortunately. But one thing I don't know, and that is what you put in your wretched envelope. May I take a look?"

"Naturally!" said Hokus.

Miss Marzipan smiled as mysteriously as a blonde sphinx. Brausewetter jumped up and leaned over behind Drinkwater's chair. This time he was trembling, not with fear, but with sheer curiosity. He was usually trembling about something or other.

The American tore open the envelope, took out a slip of paper, and unfolded it. He went rigid.

Brausewetter, who was peeping over his shoulder, rolled his eyes and whispered: "I'm going to faint." But he did not faint after all, because he just managed to grasp Mr. Drink-water's armchair, I mean his chair arm, in time. He just went a bit weak in the knees.

The movie mogul from the U.S.A. didn't notice. He just sat there rigid in his armchair, like a figure in a wax museum. For the slip of paper he had fished out of the unsealed envelope looked exactly like this:

In other words, the paper was blank! There was no figure on it. There was no signature under the figure that was not there. Nothing. It was the blankest slip of paper that was ever put into an envelope.

It was at least five minutes before the wax figure named John F. Drinkwater made a move. It blinked its eyelids. That was the first sign of life.

"He's coming around," declared Maxie.

After another two minutes the American found his tongue. "I'm a jackass," he said angrily. "I could have saved myself half of the two million, and even then you'd have been doing well. A blank sheet of paper! Your Mr. Goethe was a cunning old devil."

Hokus smiled. "Our Mr. Goethe was only half a cunning devil. The envelope idea was his, but putting absolutely nothing on the paper was my own brainwave."

"Congratulations," snarled Drinkwater. "But what if I'd written only ten or twenty thousand dollars?"

"You would never have done that," said Rosa Marzipan. "You were so absolutely set on getting the film rights."

Drinkwater nodded ruefully. "That's right, Rosie. All the same, let's suppose I'd taken the risk. I'm a fairly good poker player."

"And I'm a fairly good illusionist," stated Hokus. "Of course, we didn't know how high you would bid, because we are not businessmen. But if you'd offered us a low figure, there would have been another envelope lying on the table."

"Another envelope? How could you have made the switch so quickly?"

"Oh, you are silly!" cried Maxie, tearing his hair with glee. "It's been lying there in front of your nose all the time!"

Mr. Drinkwater looked at the table. There it was, indeed. Right in front of his nose lay a second sealed envelope. He gaped at it as if, despite his height (six and a half feet), he were a rabbit and the envelope a rattlesnake.

"Open it and look," Hokus suggested. "Take it easy!"

Mr. Drinkwater was already tearing the envelope open. He pulled the paper out and went as white as the paper. "But . . . but it's not possible! That kind of money doesn't exist!"

The Professor nodded. "If you had offered much too little, I should have demanded much too much. And then our deal—"

"Would have been off!" Maxie gleefully cried.

"And we would have waited for a more interesting offer," Rosa Marzipan added.

"You're a cunning lot, the three of you," said Drinkwater. "And if you work half as well during the filming as you've done just now, the movie'll be a masterpiece."

"It will be. What would you like to bet?" asked Maxie.

Drinkwater raised his hand in protest. "Bet? With a little thing like you? No fear. I'm not all that rich."

"But now *I* am rich," Maxie declared proudly. "May I invite you to partake of a pineapple tart?"

"Pineapple tart be blowed!"

They spent the rest of the afternoon discussing the movie, so now begins . . .

4

Operation Sleeping Beauty · Sergeant-major Mühlenschulte vaguely remembers · Bald Otto gets a thirst again · What's a piano doing swinging through the air? · Stilke's Circus visits Glasgow and London

During the night that followed these events a startling hold-up took place. It went off without a hitch. The perpetrators got away without being identified. They stole neither money nor furs nor jewels. They stole two prisoners. They did not rob a jewelry shop or a bank. They robbed a prison.

It was, of course, the most confounded effrontery. At the same time, it was something unusual. And the press, the broadcasting services, and the newsreels really went to town over this unusual event. But that was later, much too late.

The chief of police raged. The prison governor resigned. And Detective Inspector Steinbeiss threatened to resign. But what good did that do? The entire police force took the disgrace to heart.

The prison governor, Dr. Heublein, was the first to discover the raid. Six or seven hours after it happened, of course. But that was not his fault, because he did not live in the prison but in a residential suburb of the city.

It would be best if I simply tell everything as it happened. That's always the right way to do it.

Well, then. Dr. Heublein drove up to the entrance of the prison on the stroke of eight, as he did every morning, and tooted his horn three times for someone to open the gate. But no one opened it. He waited and tooted again. No one stirred. Such a thing had never happened before.

Furious, he got out of his car, stood on tiptoe, and looked through the barred window into the guardroom. At first he was struck dumb by what he saw. Then he said to himself, "It can't be!" He knocked on the window loudly. "Witschoreck!" he shouted, "what on earth do you think you're doing?"

Sergeant-major Witschoreck was seated at the desk, asleep. Beside his chair lay the Alsatian dog Diana, also asleep. Knocking on the window obviously was not going to work.

Dr. Heublein ran to the gate and pounded on the door. One of the heavy iron doors groaned. Heublein could hear the bunch of keys rattling inside. He threw himself with all the strength he could muster against the massive gate until it opened enough to allow him to stagger into the yard. Then he pushed the door shut, turned the key in the lock, and tried to get his breath back a little. But in vain.

For his eye fell upon Sergeant-major Mühlenschulte, holding the Alsatian dog Pluto by his lead; but their eyes did not fall upon him. They were sleeping peacefully on the ground.

Dr. Heublein, his knees knocking, crossed the yard to the prison. His hair stood on end. The prison block's door also stood open! He stole along the corridor. He went up and up, from one floor to the next. Everywhere the same thing. The prisoners were asleep. The prison warders were asleep. The nurses in the infirmary were asleep. The cook and her assistants were asleep. The boilerman and his pair of parakeets were asleep. And even the flies on the wall were asleep.

In a state of shock, Dr. Heublein telephoned the chief of police and stammered out the extraordinary news. The chief of police bellowed into the receiver, "It's too early for joking," But he began to think it over. Perhaps it wasn't a joke.

Ten minutes later a dozen patrol cars were racing through the city. The lights on their roofs were revolving; their sirens were wailing. Large official cars followed them. In the first one sat the chief of police himself, the chief public health officer, Dr. Grieneisen, Detective Inspector Steinbeiss, and Professor Dickhut, head of the criminal pathology laboratory. Passers-by gazed in perplexity as the cars swept by.

"Why are they in such a hurry?" asked one woman with a heavy shopping basket.

"Perhaps someone's milk boiled over," suggested the little boy standing beside her.

"My goodness gracious!" she cried in fury. "I've forgotten to turn off the gas again!" She had already turned round and was running toward the next corner.

"You appear to be a real cheeky monkey," commented a severe looking gentleman.

"Though I say it myself," the boy retorted, "I'm little, but good."

The chief of police was sitting in the guardroom declaring in a hollow voice, "This isn't a prison, it's a madhouse!" He contemplated the sleeping sergeants and the sleeping dogs. The police had dragged Sergeant-major Mühlenschulte and Pluto, former European champion, inside. After all, they could not leave them lying in the prison yard.

Chief public health officer Grieneisen and Professor Dickhut examined the two sergeants and the two dogs. Grieneisen said, "No fever. Pulse normal. Breathing regular. All four are as fit as fiddles."

"Only a wee bit tired," the chief of police commented sarcastically. "And when do you suppose this blessed prison will finally wake up? Sooner or later I've got to question someone about what happened last night!"

Dr. Heublein, the prison governor, stared out of the barred window and muttered, "Sleeping Beauty slept for a hundred years."

"We haven't got that much time!" The chief of police was croaking with exasperation. "We'll all have been pensioned off long before then!"

Then Professor Dickhut took over. He didn't care a rap for fairy tales. He was a chemist. "Our American colleagues," he began, "have developed what they call humane chemical warfare, something we know nothing of here. It could have been some kind of gas. Grenades filled with nerve gas can be shot at enemy troops, who immediately fall down and go to sleep."

"For a hundred years?"

"Oh, no, only a couple of hours or so."

"And you seriously think that last night an armored tank

with American nerve gas grenades came and bombarded the prison?"

"Not quite that, chief," said Professor Dickhut, smiling. "Nerve poisons like that can, of course, be made in various forms once they have been discovered. They can be tablets, sprays, canisters. They can be used just as gardeners use insecticides."

"I've got to take your word for it," declared the chief of police. "You are the stinks specialist. It could have happened like that. What I want to know is, why? Why would any-one transform a whole prison into a modern version of the Sleeping Beauty?"

"I know why," cried Inspector Steinbeiss breathlessly. He had just come back from the prison block and had over-heard the question. "Two prisoners have been stolen. Those two rogues who kidnapped The Little Man." Then he dashed to the telephone.

Professor Hokus von Pokus and The Little Man were sitting at breakfast in their hotel room when the telephone rang. Hokus lifted the receiver, gave his name, and then cried gaily: "Good morning, Inspector. Of course he's here. He has stickied himself all over with strawberry jam as usual. Oh, well, he's a millionaire, so I suppose he can do as he pleases. — What's happened? — Bernhard and Bald Otto disappeared? — How? — Night attack? Everybody asleep? Even the Alsatians? — Aha. A nerve gas attack. No clues? — Don't you worry. I shan't let the lad out of my sight.

What? — Certainly. It must be the work of an organized band. Have you called Tempelhof Airport? That's the most important spot. Make inquiries about chartered planes! — Right. — You'll call us back later? — Good. Thank you very much for calling."

When Hokus relayed the phone message, Maxie said, "Señor Lopez is behind all this, or I'll eat my hat."

"Fortunately it's a small size," said Hokus. "And now go wipe the jam off your face."

Maxie wiped his face. Then he asked, "Do you think they'll get their hands on me again?"

Hokus shook his head. "No, the whole lot of them are long since across the border. It was a rearguard action."

"And why has this Lopez fellow got Bernhard and Bald Otto out of prison? It was a very dangerous and very expensive thing to do, wasn't it?"

"Money's no object to that man," said Hokus and drained his coffee cup. "And which was the more dangerous for him—to spring the two crooks, or to let them come up for trial? Who knows what they might have revealed in hopes of a light sentence."

"I get it," said Maxie. "That's the way it must have been. And I'm glad I won't have to eat my hat."

The first sleeper to awaken was the European champion Alsatian, Pluto. He opened his jaws wide, but only to yawn. Alsatians may be intelligent beasts, but they are not great talkers.

The next to come to life was Sergeant-major Mühlen-schulte. He suddenly opened his eyes, looked about him and said, "Huh." It wasn't much of a speech either. But the chief of police made him swallow a pint of black coffee. That helped.

He began to remember. "Witschoreck and I were having a game of checkers when the bell on the gate rang. So I went with Pluto and my bunch of keys, opened the spyhole and saw a man in a black, high-necked get-up. He claimed he was the representative of the prison chaplains' union and that he had been called because the prisoner in cell 34 wanted to confess an armed robbery to him."

"What rubbish!" cried Dr. Heublein exasperatedly.

"You took the words right out of my mouth, Doctor. 'What rubbish,' I told him. Then he pushed a flexible metal tube through the open spyhole. I just thought, 'Surely he's not going to demonstrate a vacuum cleaner . . . in the middle of the night . . . at the prison gates . . .' And . . ."

"Well?" asked Dr. Grieneisen.

"I remember nothing more," declared Mühlenschulte. "Complete blackout. I'm sorry." He started. "Witschoreck! What are you doing sleeping there? Gustav! Wake up, will you!"

But Sergeant Witschoreck had not yet gotten that far.

At about the same time Bald Otto opened his eyes, and they nearly popped out of his head. He was sitting in a plane. The morning sun was shining. The sky was a brilliant steely blue. They were flying over white clouds like a hundred thousand of the finest featherbeds. "Funny," he thought. "This doesn't look like jail to me."

Then someone next to him said, "A very good morning to you. Had a good sleep?"

Otto gazed suspiciously at his neighbor, then grinned from ear to ear. "Boileau, old pal, how did you get here?"

"It would be more reasonable to ask how *you* got here," said Monsieur Boileau.

"One thing at a time. First of all, a drop of brandy, if you don't mind. Or is this a 'dry' plane?" After the third glass he felt livelier. "And what about Bernhard? Is he on board too?"

"Yes, but he's still asleep."

"Pity," said Bald Otto. "What I mean is, pity you didn't leave him behind in the jug. Boy, can he be nasty when he likes! He treated me like dirt, he did. I don't stand for that kind of thing. Let me out of here, I'll fix him!"

"Don't get excited," Boileau warned him. "Think of your blood pressure!"

"Thinking's not my line," said Otto.

Boileau nodded. "Glad you've seen the light at last. Your stupidity is costing the Chief a lot of money. Letting yourself be conned by a whippersnapper only two inches tall! You get nabbed. Our colleague Ballhaus radios Lopez. Lopez radios me. I hire a plane and a couple of dozen specialists. We take a trip to Berlin, put a prison to sleep, risk life and limb—what's it all in aid of? Merely to get a couple of slowpokes like you out of your own rotten mess!"

"Shut up, will you!" someone shouted angrily. It was Bernhard. He had awakened and overheard Boileau's complaints. "And don't try to tell us that Lopez sent you after us just because he loves us so much. He was scared that Otto would let the cat out of the bag. He'd sell his own grandmother for a glass of brandy."

"Do me a favor, will you, and get a bit more shuteye," growled Bald Otto. "Why didn't you just leave the rat in

his cell? I can't stand that kind of talk. Especially on an empty stomach."

"Are you hungry?" Boileau asked.

"I sure am."

"Sandwich?"

"No, a couple of glasses of brandy," Otto suggested. "I'm not on solids yet. I'm still on liquids."

Meanwhile, the police department had not been idle. Inspector Steinbeiss had located the hangar at Tempelhof Airport from which the chartered plane had flown off into the night. But the plane had not touched down in Paris. It had gone elsewhere, into the blue.

The news reporters, too, were no slouches. All that they knew and didn't know was already in the newspapers that were on sale in the streets that afternoon. The reports were all over the front pages. Gigantic headlines read: OPERATION SLEEPING BEAUTY!

When Inspector Steinbeiss read the newspapers, he turned green with annoyance. Most people turn yellow with annoyance. But he always turned green, a completely new reaction. But there was worse to come.

Two hours later his wife telephoned his office. She was beside herself, shouting and crying and raging at him so much that he had to hold the receiver away from his ear so she wouldn't split his eardrums. "Have you gone crazy?" she yelled at the top of her voice. "What do we want with a piano?"

"A piano?" He gripped the edge of his desk.

"Yes, a piano! They couldn't get it up the stairs and now they're bringing a block and tackle to hoist it up the outside wall and get it through the window!"

"But Fanny," Inspector Steinbeiss cried, "I didn't order any piano!"

"Yes you did, *and* paid for it!" she shrieked. "They showed me the bill! And as if buying a piano wasn't enough! Why did you send people here to rent our apartment? They think we're moving out!"

Inspector Steinbeiss took a deep breath.

"And there was an ambulance here too," she screamed. "They wanted to take away your nephew—they said he'd broken his leg in our bathroom!"

"For goodness' sake pull yourself together," he said calmly. "I'm coming home right away. And don't leave the apartment!"

"I can't get out anyway! There are ten big cases of wine vinegar piled outside! Why in creation did you order ten cases of wine vinegar?"

Inspector Steinbeiss hung up and jammed his hat on his head.

When he turned into Konstanz Street, he saw in the distance a great crowd of people collected outside his house. High in the air an upright piano was dangling. Frau Steinbeiss— otherwise Fanny—a plump and usually very placid person, was leaning out of an open window on the third floor with

her hands stretched out to prevent delivery of the instrument.

And there were not just idlers and inquisitive passers-by on the pavement! Oh, no. Press photographers, cameramen, and reporters were there too. They were photographing and shooting film, taking notes, interviewing bystanders, and laughing so loudly that one couldn't hear oneself think.

Steinbeiss leaped out of his car.

"Here comes the big shot, at last!" one reporter called out.

"What are you doing here?" he demanded angrily.

"Steady on!" replied the newspaperman, and he was honestly offended. "You yourself invited us all here! Who else would have called us up and told us we could get a story outside your house?"

"If it wasn't you, then it must have been someone who has it in for you," was the opinion of a press photographer. "A piano in midair, your wife at the window, pictures in all the newspapers and newsreels, with snappy captions and commentaries . . .''

Inspector Steinbeiss dashed up the stairs, clambered over the cases of wine vinegar and pounded on the door with his fists until Fanny opened up. Then he ran to the telephone, called a radio patrol car to his aid, and finally had himself put on to the chief of police. "Chief," he announced, "I'm handing in my resignation."

"I know all about it already," the chief of police replied. "Think nothing of it, old boy. No one's a match for this Señor Lopez. I would never dream of giving up the services of such a first-class man as yourself. But I'll give you a six-month leave of absence. Then we'll see. O.K?"

"Okay," said Inspector Steinbeiss. "And even if I have to swim the Atlantic to do it, I'll get my hands on that Señor Lopez!"

That evening Inspector Steinbeiss was sitting with Mr. Drinkwater in the lounge of the Hilton Hotel. The American made the Inspector go over every detail of Operation Sleeping Beauty, the sparse reports from Interpol, and the unwanted gift of a piano. "And how can I help you?" he asked.

"I must find this Lopez," Steinbeiss declared. "He played me for a sucker. No man alive can do that to me and get away with it. Today I'm the laughingstock of the whole world. What I want is to see the world laughing at him, and pronto!"

"I can understand that," said Drinkwater. "So you want to fly to South America."

"That's right."

"And get in touch with the police over there."

"No. Anyone as rich as Lopez will certainly have friends among the police. They would warn him of my arrival, and I would be taken for a ride again."

"Then who's going to help you?"

"You."

"Me?"

"Listen," said the Inspector. "You send a film unit to the region where we think Lopez is hiding out. No one notices that a couple of detectives from New York and Detective Inspector Steinbeiss from Berlin are among the crew. We behave like working members of the unit. We go as truck-drivers, food contractors, tent erectors. My friend Mackintosh from New York acts as interpreter. He knows South America like the palm of his hand and is one of the cleverest detectives under the sun. The unit is supposed to be shooting an art documentary about the land and its people, their customs, festivals, educational system, its plants and exotic butterflies . . ."

"I can just see it," said Drinkwater, shuddering, "a ghastly flop. But I know the sort of thing you mean."

"We shoot a few cockatoos and parrots, and all the time we're pumping the locals. It's absolutely certain that this Lopez will have some enemies. We'll find his fortress . . ."

"That kind of expedition costs a tidy penny. It could very

easily come to grief. But if we get only a hundred feet of usable film in the can, I'll finance the whole thing."

"I can't promise anything," said the Inspector. "I have a bit of money in the bank, and I can get a loan on my life insurance."

"Either I don't take on a project of that nature," Drinkwater drily retorted, "or I take the whole risk upon myself. That's what I intend to do. When are you leaving?"

"The day after tomorrow."

"Good. Cable your friend Mackintosh. I'll inform my New York office. The film unit's expedition will be arranged there. I'll let you know further details tomorrow morning. How does your wife feel about it?"

"She's going to her sister's," said the Inspector, "because now she doesn't dare leave the house. Everybody's laughing at us. Yesterday morning, I found chalked on the wall of our house: 'Piano lessons given here from today, for four hands, by Detective Inspector Steinbeiss (retired) and spouse. Apply 3rd Floor.' We disconnected the doorbell and had our telephone changed to an unlisted number. We just couldn't stand it any longer."

"This Lopez is a wicked prankster," said Mr. Drinkwater. "But who are his cronies over here? Who paid for that piano? Who ordered the ambulance? And the ten cases of wine vinegar?"

"The police are baffled. All false names and addresses were given. Only the money was real."

"Who chartered the plane? Who was the leader of that

tourist group? Who was the pilot? How was Operation Sleeping Beauty planned down to the last detail? Where did the plane carrying Bald Otto and Bernhard fly to from Tempelhof?"

"The police don't know a thing. In Paris they know as little about it as we do. Our laboratory has analysed the chemical structure of the spray that put the entire prison to sleep, but that doesn't get us anywhere. What can we do with a chemical formula?"

Mr. Drinkwater sprang up. "Into battle!" he said. "Pack your bags!"

Two days later Inspector Steinbeiss flew to New York, and we shall be hearing nothing of him for a longish period.

Mr. Drinkwater frequently visited Stilke's Circus and took more notes. Even more frequently he paid visits to Maxie, Hokus, and Rosa Marzipan at their hotel. Jakob Hurtig, the schoolboy, was often there with them. Mostly they discussed the film they intended to shoot in Munich in October and November.

Jakob was to be excused from school for a few weeks in order to play his part in the movie. "I'm delighted as a dog with two tails," he said. "It'll be the film of the century. Why doesn't October hurry up and come along?"

"Because it's only a few days since you were spitting cherrystones into the street," said Maxie. "Don't get the calendar all topsy-turvy!"

Munich was still a long way off. In August Stilke's Circus played the Kelvin Hall in Glasgow, way up north in Scotland. In September it appeared in London at the Olympia. Even *The Times* said that its success was unprecedented. "Maxie the First Wonder of the Modern World," ran one headline.

It was not until the end of September that things really started moving. Once more the circus folk embarked with their animals. Once more a freight train loaded with trailers and cages went rattling through the night. Once more they crossed the English channel by cargo boat, this time from Harwich to Hook of Holland. Once more a giraffe, the haute école rider Galoppinski, and Ali the lion were seasick. Once more the train rattled on through Holland. But this time the destination was Munich! And so begins . . .

Press conference in Munich · The village on wheels · Maxie puts a woman reporter in her place · Haute école rider Galopinski has to ask his horse's permission · Five portions of caramel pudding are too much · What about a trip to Pichelstein?

A circus like Stilke's is, as I have pointed out, no small matter. And the circus manager's life is no joke. The nearest comparison he can make with himself is that of town mayor, but in all towns and villages there are only human beings and nice domesticated animals, no lions, tigers, elephants, bears, apes, or sea lions at all.

A second important difference springs to mind: the circus is a traveling village. Every month or every other month they live in a different place. Overnight the village is suddenly dismantled. Then the next day, or at the most, two days later, the very same village comes into being on the outskirts of another city, perhaps in another country, where they speak a different language. And on that very evening the first performance takes place. It's like magic.

But there's no magic involved, only hard work. Every movement is planned. Every man functions like a cog in a machine. The man in charge of loading and unloading, the director of the menagerie, the tentmaster, the parking-lot supervisor, and the chief electrician are the largest cogs in the organization. And who has to keep the whole complicated clockwork ticking in his head yet keep his hair on? The ringmaster. The mayor of the village on wheels. That's why he needs nerves of steel. Or at least many pairs of gray and black gloves.

The journey from London to Munich went as smoothly as a dream. When Brausewetter received the press in the Krone Circus building, he was sporting white gloves, and his moustache was standing at ten minutes past ten o'clock.

He started with a brief outline. "Ladies and gentlemen," he said, "we are a village on wheels. One hundred and fifty workmen and artistes live in caravans with their families.

They look after themselves and even cook themselves."

"Well, I never!" cried a young woman in hornrimmed glasses with a reporter's pad. "They even cook *themselves?* Does it taste good?"

Brausewetter shook a white-clad forefinger at her. "Now don't you take everything I say too literally, young lady! I shall give you a few figures and nothing more. For our 300 animals alone we have to purchase 300 pounds of meat, 40 pounds of bread, 200 pounds of fruit and vegetables, 45 pints of milk, 72 cubic feet of sawdust, and 36 cubic feet of soil *every day*. For the parking area we need 100 gallons of fuel per day, and for the lighting equipment and heating, 150 gallons of fuel oil."

"For crying out loud," remarked one journalist, "that's what I would call an expensive sort of treat."

Brausewetter nodded vigorously. "And if we're not sold out every evening, it's no treat at all, just expensive, because my employees' hunger can't be adjusted to the sale of tickets at the box office. Every day they consume, for example, a hundredweight of bread, a hundredweight of potatoes, and half a hundredweight of meat."

"And how much does The Little Man consume?" another journalist asked. "Our readers are most eager to find out."

The ringmaster pointed to the door. Professor Hokus von Pokus and Mr. Drinkwater had just entered. "Ask him yourselves!"

The journalists and the forward young miss jumped up and applauded. Maxie, ensconced in the Professor's breast pocket, was waving to them. When they had all sat down again, the reporter repeated his question.

"How much do I eat and drink in a day?" Maxie reflected briefly. "Well, I couldn't tell you to the exact millimeter. Sometimes it's a bit more and sometimes a bit less, just the same as with people who are thirty to forty times taller than I am. But approximately I should say I consume about a couple of square centimeters of brown bread, a knifepoint of butter, a teaspoonful of cocoa, a thimbleful of lemonade, one small button mushroom, three cubic centimeters of veal cutlet or filet mignon, one tenth of a new potato, two morsels of sausage . . ."

"What! No cheese?" exclaimed the forward young miss.

"Oh, yes, yes. But only Swiss cheese. Lots of it, though! Every day twenty to thirty holes!"

They all laughed at that. Except the young woman.

The press conference went on for another solid hour. First Hokus spoke to the assembled journalists, and finally it was Mr. Drinkwater's turn. He talked about the film he was going to shoot, about the difficulties of photographing a circus, particularly the big top, around which The Little Man was to fly on the back of Emma, the dove, about the sequences to be shot in Studio 5 out at Geiselgasteig, and about the location shots in Pichelstein, where not one of the inhabitants is more than twenty inches tall. That curious little village that Maxie's parents had left one day in order to seek fame and fortune as circus artistes.

"Do you still remember anything about Pichelstein?" the obnoxious young miss inquired.

"No," replied Maxie. "I was never there." He could not bear the silly goose. He found her distinctly repulsive.

"But surely you must remember your cute little parents," she went on in honeyed tones. "And how you felt when you were told that they had been blown off the Eiffel Tower. And surely you remember how the two artificial Chinese pigtails were laid to rest? Did you cry very much?"

Maxie was silent. The others sat there stiff with embarrassment.

"Why don't you answer me?" the pert young thing asked impatiently.

"He doesn't answer because you are a tactless person," Hokus said quietly.

"What's tact got to do with it?" She tapped her ballpoint pen on the table. "A good reporter shouldn't be too sensitive. Well, Little Man, what about it?"

Maxie nodded. "Right you are, madam." He had already jumped on to the table top. In a flash he had scrambled up to her head. The next minute he was standing right in the middle of her elaborately teased hairdo, tugging and tearing at it for all he was worth.

"Ouch!" She gave a piercing shriek. "Let go!" she screamed. "Don't just stand there, everybody, *do* something! Help! Help!"

No one stirred so much as a little finger. She waved her hands like a windmill, but Maxie was not to be deterred. He really made hay of her beehive. The hair went flying in fist-fuls through the air. She squawked. She bawled. She yelled in torment. But Maxie was merciless. The news photographers' lights flashed. It was a crazy scene.

The young woman was almost unrecognizable. The elaborate hairdo was in ruins. Tears of rage had made her eye make-up run all over. In a last desperate effort the young woman struck at her head in order to knock Maxie away, but she only hit herself and a hairpin, which made her howl with pain. The mascara burned her eyes. She could no longer see a thing. Her torn hair hung down in lank strands over her shoulders. She looked ghastly.

Maxie had long ago returned to the safety of Hokus's breast pocket. He was still panting for breath. "There!" he said at last. "And now I shall give you your answer. Yes, at that time I did cry, very much."

Mr. Drinkwater was an outstanding organizer—a real "old movie hand," as they call such an experienced man in film circles. No one could put anything over on him—neither cameramen, nor sound engineers, nor production assistants, nor production managers, nor lighting experts. He carried in his head the final plans for the TV series and the film of *The Little Man* as clearly as if they had been engraved upon his brain. Each day's tasks were completed as he had intended. There were no breakdowns. No excuses were accepted.

Every evening, together with his most important collaborators, he looked at the "rushes" in the projection room. Rushes are the reels of film that have been developed in the processing laboratory. Beside him sat the film cutter, whom he told where and how the scenes should be cut and what sections should be incorporated in the finished movie.

He himself could stand this drudgery from morn till night without a pause. His crew were dead beat by the time evening came. But they pulled themselves together. He was the chief. He was the boss. "The man's got real drive," they would tell each other wonderingly. He was the locomotive that hauled everything and everyone along after him.

He and Hokus got on marvelously. From the first day of shooting they were using each other's first names. However, the Professor seldom called the long drink of water John. He often called him Johannes and even more often Johnny.

Maxie and all the other circus people went through their parts very well. The only difficulty was with the haute école rider, because he would neither wear the conjurer's tailcoat nor allow himself to be thrown from his steed in front of the cameras.

"It goes against my professional principles," Maestro Galoppinski declared proudly. "The film will be shown all over the world, and Nero and I would suffer a permanent loss of reputation." Nero was his black stallion.

Even when Mr. Drinkwater offered him a higher salary and the horse two extra hundredweight of sugar cubes, the pair remained stubborn and immovable. The situation had reached an impasse. Mr. Drinkwater was thinking of cabling the cowboy star Tom Middleton, to find out whether he and his lily-white steed Moonlight had time to play in the movie, when Hokus broke into the discussion.

"Professional principles must be respected," he declared. "But I know Tom Middleton and his white horse. Both are excellent performers. Nevertheless my dear Galoppinski, Tom and Moonlight are simply not in the same international class as you and Nero. Tom is not elegant enough. He'll fall from his horse like a sack of coals, and his white horse will be so highly strung that he'll stampede not out of the ring but into the boxes."

"I'm afraid you're right, dear Professor Hokus von Pokus," said the rider. "But it can't be helped. Only once in our lives did Nero and I make fools of each other. That was in Berlin, when all unawares I put on your crazy tails. We're still suffering from the shame of that occasion. And you want us to repeat that disgrace deliberately, in a movie and on TV? And have everyone from Washington to Moscow and from Buenos Aires to Hong Kong laughing themselves silly over us? No, gentlemen. Not for all the cubes of sugar in the world!"

Hokus and Mr. Drinkwater hung their heads.

Suddenly Maxie called out, "I have it!"

They all jumped, because their troubles had made them forget he was in the Professor's breast pocket, listening to all that was going on.

66

"I have it!" repeated Maxie, rubbing his hands together with glee. "They sell programs in every movie theater. We could print in the programs how difficult it had been for Herr Galoppinski to tumble off Nero because both are in the front rank of international performers and therefore could hardly be expected to do such a thing. Therefore they had to practice the fall for months on end. Like clowns."

"I don't like to be laughed to scorn," Galoppinski said. He was a little embarrassed.

"Since when have clowns been laughed to scorn?" asked Mr. Drinkwater. "Every child in the circus knows that they are not clumsy but only pretend to be so. One does not laugh them to scorn. One laughs *for* them because they themselves remain serious."

Maestro Galoppinski was a horseman and no thinker, and without his horse he was, as it were, only half there. So he stood up suddenly and muttered, "I need time to think it over," and marched towards the door.

"Now where are you off to?" asked Mr. Drinkwater.

"To the stables." And he was gone.

"What's he going to do in the stables?"

"He's going to ask the horse about it," said Maxie. "He and Nero do everything together."

"Don't try to tell me the beast can talk!"

"No, but he can listen," said Hokus. "After Galoppinski has spoken to him, the horse looks at him. Nothing more. But it's enough to tell Galoppinski whether Nero has understood him or not."

"They always do it that way," added Maxie.

Mr. Drinkwater was dumbfounded.

Five minutes later Galoppinski came back from the stables. "Everything's fixed," he declared. "My horse has no objection."

Weeks of very hard work followed. Every evening and three afternoons a week there were circus performances. Every morning at seven they had to be at the film studio. The make-up men were there, ready with their make-up boxes. When the make-up man painted Maxie's face, he had to use a large magnifying glass.

On sound stage 5 various sets had been constructed: a hotel room, a hotel corridor, a display window containing Winsome Waldemar and other tailor's dummies, the interior of the gentlemen's outfitters, the kidnappers' room, Jakob

Hurtig's ground-floor window, his parents' living room, the Detective Inspector's office, the Blue Salon, Brausewetter's caravan, and heaven knows what else. It was like being at a fair. They shot for two days in the Blue Salon, three days in the kidnappers' hideout, and half a day in the dining room of The Loaded Dice, in which the actress who played the owner of the place had to throw caramel pudding into the face of the actor playing Bernhard.

Because it was hard to get the lighting exactly right, this scene had to be shot four times. By the time he had the third pudding plonked in his face, the actor was in a tearing rage. But Mr. Drinkwater would not give up until his cameraman expressed himself satisfied with the fourth take.

At midday they all ate in the canteen. There they all were —the two kidnappers sitting happily together with Rosa, Hokus, and the actor playing Inspector Steinbeiss. Maxie stood beside Jakob Hurtig's plate and sampled the liver-and-dumpling soup. Mr. Drinkwater chatted with the unshaven actor playing Bald Otto. The manageress of the studio canteen served the actress who had just been playing the manageress of The Loaded Dice. And everybody had a good laugh.

But the loudest laughter of all came that day when dessert was served. Naturally, the actor playing Bernhard did not join in the laughter. He screamed with horror. For what do you think was served up to him for dessert? Caramel pudding with raspberry sauce!

Four puddings plonked in his face and then a fifth shoved

under his nose was definitely too much for him. He calmed down only when the canteen manageress brought him Camembert and pumpernickel instead of the wibbly-wobbly pudding.

Maxie worked like a Trojan. The film was a great joke to him. But he also liked watching when he was not in front of the cameras. He would often clamber up the cameraman and was allowed to look through the viewfinder, even when the camera was tracking or was being hoisted by a crane.

One October evening after viewing the day's rushes, when the four of them were sitting in the restaurant called The Little Brown Jug, Mr. Drinkwater said, "Tomorrow morning early, at six o'clock, I shall be taking the car to Pichelstein. The chief cameraman is already there. The studio crew will travel tonight. If the weather tomorrow's the same as it has been this lovely, bright autumn day, we'll be shooting outside by midday. Otherwise, we'll shoot in the gymnasium. The Pichelstein Amateur Gymnastics Association will be showing off its paces: exercises on the floor, high bar, rings, horseback, the wall racks, and the balancing beam. These will be the movie's opening shots."

He paused a second, smiled, and asked, "Would you like to come along?"

"Wouldn't I just!" breathed Maxie.

"And what's going to become of Stilke's Circus?" Hokus wanted to know.

"You'll come back by car in time for the performance," said Drinkwater. "I will remain in Pichelstein during the shooting. However, I shall have to spend the night in Regensburg because the beds in the Pichelstein Inn are too short for me. The longest they have measures only two foot four, so they'd have to put three of their beds end to end to accommodate me. But they haven't a big enough room for that."

"Of course we're coming with you," declared Rosa Marzipan firmly. "The boy ought to get to know his parents' home town."

"Will you be all right, Maxie?" Hokus asked anxiously.

Maxie gazed back at him undecidedly. "I'd like to go very much," he said, "but I feel a little bit scared about it."

"But we shall be with you," said the Professor.

"Yes, of course. Otherwise . . . nothing but people called Pichelsteiner, and all related to me, and all trying to tell me how they used to go to school with my parents . . . "

Early the next morning as they drove out of Munich it was still dark and misty. Later, as it grew lighter, the mist melted away, and in Regensburg the sun was already shining brightly. The sky was like blue silk. The trees were ablaze with brilliant autumn tints. Beyond Regensburg they drove along narrow country roads. They climbed into the mountains through meadows and woods.

"Pichelstein lies up there," said Mr. Drinkwater's chauffeur. And here begins . . .

▫ 6 ▫

"Warning: when visiting the church and the City Hall,
watch your head!" · *When did the Giant Circle become hereditary?*
Maxie's parents impersonated · *Inspector Steinbeiss returns*
from South America · *Senor Lopez is captured, but only on film,*
and then takes flight!

There was a notice at the side of the road. They stopped to read it: "Warning! No Through Traffic! Parking lot outside the town! Accommodation only for children no taller than 20 inches! When visiting church & City Hall, watch your heads! We ask for your kind cooperation! Welcome to Pichelstein! Alois Pichelsteiner, Mayor."

Rosa Marzipan burst out laughing. "We'd better go down on our hands and knees. I only hope the streets are wide enough for us."

"That's all right for us men," said Hokus. "But for you . . ."

"Don't be so cheeky," said Rosa, "or I'll call off our engagement."

Then they fell silent and looked excitedly to their right. Through the autumnal stubblefields rumbled a tiny farm wagon drawn by a tiny pony. The wagon was no bigger than a handcart, and the farmer looked like a boy in his first year at school. But he had gray hair. He waved to the people in the car as he turned off the field path and into the highway.

"Looks just like a children's carriage at the zoo," said Mr. Drinkwater.

"Your father was just the same size as that old farmer," Hokus told Maxie, who was watching the little wagon moving away.

The boy was sitting on the Professor's shoulder, gazing out over the little rectangles of the meadows and the freshly ploughed fields to right and left. He did not reply.

"I wonder if the potatoes here are as big as they are where we come from?" asked the chauffeur. "If so, the potato harvest must be back-breaking work for them."

Finally Maxie spoke. "Now I suppose that two of the people in the village will be used in the film to impersonate my parents."

The reception was held in the parking area, after the guests had gotten out of the car.

The Fire Brigade band, composed entirely of tiny men with tiny musical instruments, blazed away with the Pichelsteiner March of the Midgets. The jubilation of the inhabitants, small though they were, was gigantic. Alois Pichelsteiner, the mayor, made a majestic speech of welcome. Ferdinand Pichelsteiner, the president of the Amateur Gymnastics Association, made Maxie an honorary member. Mr. Drinkwater handed the mayor, as a token of thanks for the community's cooperation in the making of the film, a check drawn on the Bank of Germany. And Ferdinand

Pichelsteiner announced that he wished to present Maxie with a gift that would always remind him of the Pichelstein A.G.A. (founded 1872).

"We have been a gymnastic-minded community for almost a hundred years," he declared. "Your beloved parents were our leaders and trainers in the gymnastic arts. They carried out into the wide, wide world the skill that has made us famous. You, honorable member, have inherited and enriched their talent. What better or more beautiful gift could we make you than gymnastic equipment? The locksmith Fidelis Pichelsteiner and my humble self have constructed for you a high bar of the finest steel with four replaceable horizontal bars, suited to your size. It is accompanied by a soft felt carpet, four inches square, so that you won't break any bones when practicing the 'long upstart,' the 'giant circle,' and the 'straddle.' Your parents were gymnasts long before you became an artiste. You are an artiste: now we want you to become a gymnast, as befits a Pichelsteiner.

The Fire Brigade band played a fanfare. The Pichelsteiners yelled "Bravo." And around the corner came a cart drawn by a donkey. On the cart stood a tiny table, and on the table the small high-bar apparatus had been set up. Everyone stared; then everyone applauded.

Maxie bowed low out of the Professor's breast pocket and cried, "Beloved namesakes, beloved friends of my parents! We thank you for this festive reception, and I thank you for this wonderful gift. I shall always treasure your high bar. But first I must just try it out to see whether the size is right.

We artistes have to be very thorough, you know." And before they knew what was happening, The Little Man was hanging full length from the horizontal bar!

The donkey pricked up his long ears. He felt ill at ease because he could not see what was going on behind him. But he kept as still as a statue—a statue with its ears in the air.

Maxie hung there motionless for a while. Then he slowly raised his legs to a horizontal position, brought his feet from their extended forward position by bending his knees and bringing them through his arms, then shoving his legs up vertically. Then he swung forward, then backward, made an uprise and then a complete forward circle of the bar on his middle. He paused briefly, supported on the high bar, to change the position of his fingers. "This is just great!" he cried to Hokus, who, terrified, had knelt down beside the little cart.

"Are you going completely crazy?" said Hokus. "Come down from there at once!"

"Just a few seconds more. I like it so much. Please put your hand out." And before Hokus could pluck him from the high bar, Maxie swung through the air once again. High, higher, highest! Arms and legs fully stretched! And suddenly he was doing a giant circle, then a second, then a third. He went rotating round the bar like the second hand on a watch. Then he did a handstand on the vibrating steel bar, yelled "Yippee!" and sprang, with straddled legs, into the palm of Hokus's outstretched hand. He even did the concluding kneebend perfectly.

"He sets my nerves on edge," Rosa Marzipan declared, in great agitation. But no one heard her, for the entire populace of Pichelstein was applauding. Ferdinand Pichelsteiner made his way to the cart and asked, "Where did he learn to do that?"

"Nowhere," answered Hokus, who was stuffing The Little Man back into the safety of his breast pocket.

"His parents could do it, of course," said Ferdinand Pichel-steiner. "But when did the giant circle become hereditary?"

Maxie giggled. "I watched them doing it on TV. The Tokyo Olympics. The Russian and Japanese work in heavy gymnastics is fabulous."

"The straddle dismount from the high bar cannot be learned from watching television," declared Chief Gymnast Ferdinand firmly.

"I learned it that way," Maxie stated. "I am an artiste."

"I know that," said Ferdinand Pichelsteiner. "I know that all too well, my boy. You are indeed a world-famous artiste. But you must have inherited your gift for gymnastics. It can't be explained in any other way. You have giant circles in the blood, so to speak."

It was an interesting day. And it was an exhausting day. The streets were too narrow. The houses were too small. Mr. Drinkwater often had to hold on to the roof gutters; he could look right into the windows of the upper stories. The camera crew had no room for their equipment in the gym-nasium. They had to shoot the gymnastic display put on by the men's and women's sections from outside, through the window that faced the Market Square.

There, on the Market Square, lunch was served to the guests. There was Pichelstein Beef on the menu. That was only natural. Other things were not so natural. The chairs were too low and fragile for the guests, the plates and spoons too tiny. They had to sit on the tables instead of on the chairs,

and they had to spoon their food out of soup tureens with soup ladles. But things went off fairly well.

Shooting began again in the afternoon. Since the sun was still shining, Mr. Drinkwater decided to film a few important street scenes. After he had arranged all the details with the cameraman, he took Rosa Marzipan to one side and told her quietly, "Go for a long walk with Hokus and Maxie."

"What for?" asked Rosa. "We want to watch the filming."

"It would be better if you took a walk," Drinkwater advised her, "because now I'm going to film the scene in which Maxie's parents say farewell to their neighbors and leave the village to try their luck in the wide, wide world."

"I understand."

"The young man and woman whom we have chosen to play the two parts look very like Maxie's parents. And their make-up is so accurately copied from old photographs of the pair that Maxie might get a nasty shock. After all, the kid was all of six years old when he lost his parents, and he has seen their photographs too . . . "

"Do you know what, Johnny?" said Rosa Marzipan. "You're even nicer than I thought you were."

"I'd rather have approached Hokus about it. Only, Maxie is perched in his breast pocket, and . . . "

"Don't give it another thought. I'll take my fiancé tramping round the fields of Pichelstein until he's ready to drop."

But that was easier said than done. For a while Hokus and Maxie enjoyed their ramble round the countryside. Then they got fed up. They began to grumble.

And however meaningfully Miss Marzipan winked at Hokus, for once in his life he failed to understand the language of the eyes. She only succeeded in making Maxie suspicious. "Why is your good lady winking away so hard?" he asked inquisitively.

"Beats me," said Hokus. "Women are known to be puzzling creatures. Even to conjurers."

"I want to watch the filming," Maxie pouted. "I know what stubblefields look like."

And so they turned back. Rosa Marzipan had no alternative but to go along with them. "Let's hope that Drinkwater's already got the scene with the parent substitutes in the can," she said to herself. But her hopes were vain.

They wandered right into the middle of the scene. The camera was mounted on an electric trolley. It was tracking slowly backwards in front of the little couple, who were laden with bags and baggage, as they tripped down the narrow street.

The young woman was pretty as a picture. The young man had a splendid black moustache. They were no taller than a couple of five-year-olds and had trouble carrying their luggage.

Little Pichelsteiners stood in doorways and leaned out of windows, waving and shouting, "Good luck!" and "All the best!" and "Send us a picture postcard!" and "Mind you don't forget us!"

The couple wanted to wave back, but they were too laden down with bags and bundles. All they could do was smile and nod to the others, and even that seemed to cause them

difficulty. For the future that lay before them belonged to the Land of Uncertainty, and it's not easy to smile when entering the unknown.

Hokus froze. Now he understood why Rosa had taken him and Maxie for a walk round the fields. He also understood why she had kept on winking at him.

"Women are known to be puzzling creatures," she hissed, looking at him reproachfully.

What about Maxie? He stared transfixed at his imitation parents. Then he gave a deep sob and said, "Dear Hokus, take me away from here! Quickly!"

Everything has an end. That applies to filming too. By the middle of November it was all over. The cameramen had everything "in the can," as they say. They had completed the shooting of the life story of The Little Man. They marched through the rain out of the studio across the countryside to the comfortably warm and cosy canteen, where they all knocked back glasses of lager.

To go with the drinks there were plates of roast pork with dumplings and fresh green salad. Mr. Drinkwater, their boss, had invited them to this feast. It was his treat. He thanked them, praised them, and then went into the next room, where others were awaiting him. For a film is not composed simply of reels of exposed celluloid.

In the next room sat—as well as Hokus, Rosa Marzipan, and Maxie—sound-track engineer Sohnemann, master cutter

Wegehenkel, and Mademoiselle Odette. The last was the continuity girl. She came from Geneva and was fluent in five languages; she spoke all five as if they were her mother tongue. It was fantastic.

Mr. Drinkwater stuck one of his big black cigars in the corner of his mouth and said, "If people's ears were as sharp as their eyes, we should now be able to sit down with the camera crew and join in the fun. But the ears are not as clever as the eyes."

"Is that so?" Maxie asked.

Hokus nodded. "Not nearly so clever. The eye understands everything it sees. But the ear understands only English or Japanese or Portuguese."

"That's not true!" Maxie cried. "Mademoiselle Odette understands five languages."

Mademoiselle Odette laughed. "There are more than five, I assure you. There are hundreds."

"Five's enough for me," said Mr. Drinkwater. "And that's still four too many. But I can't help that. I'm no ear doctor but a businessman. I don't want to change the world. I want to make films that can be understood everywhere, so that I can sell them everywhere." Thereupon he laid on the table the timetable for the dubbing studio he had rented and began to go into technical details about versions and "takes" and directions for the music cues and superimpositions and how many copies were to be made.

The discussion lasted three hours, and you wouldn't have understood one tenth of what they were saying. You're lucky not to have been there. The canteen manageress remained standing in the open door after she had switched on the lights. But then she shrugged her shoulders and went back to the kitchen and said to the cook, "It's all double Dutch to me."

"Well, what d'you expect?" the cook calmly replied. "Some people make films, other people make dumplings. As long as everyone knows his own job, that's the main thing. You can't expect more than that."

At seven in the evening Mr. Drinkwater was still talking. He seemed, as usual, to be tireless. "On November thirtieth, I shall fly to Genoa to board my yacht *Sleepwell*, and I won't be available for a whole month. Don't let me have any blooper in the copying of the TV series!" he cried. "The first episode goes out over thirty channels on Christmas day. Anyone who makes a blooper will have me to reckon with!"

"But not before you've had your sleep out," remarked Herr Wegehenkel. And Herr Sohnemann added, "So not before January first. At least we shall be able to celebrate New Year's Eve in peace."

Drinkwater commented darkly, "It would be your last." And because Maxie laughed and Rosa Marzipan burst into giggles, he went on even more threateningly, "I fear that the present company does not take me seriously." At that, everybody burst out laughing. For they were very fond of the long American drink of water, and they knew that he knew it.

Just then the door burst open. A taxi driver dumped two

suitcases in the room, growled, "Evening, all!" and disappeared. Then for a while nothing happened.

Finally they heard heavy footsteps. A suntanned man suddenly appeared in the open doorway. And Maxie cried out, "Why, it's Detective Inspector Steinbeiss!"

After hearty greetings they went to the projection room to watch the color film that the Inspector had brought from South America. It was a short film with no soundtrack. As soon as the ceiling lights had been extinguished and the screen illuminated, Herr Steinbeiss explained what they were seeing.

"On this lofty and remote plateau you are looking at," he began, "there is a subtropical climate. It is a fertile land, helped by artificial irrigation. People plant and harvest sugar cane, cotton, grapes, bananas, and figs, and also potatoes, wheat, maize, and barley. The peasants are descendants of the Araucos, an Indian tribe that in earlier days made life difficult for the Incas, and, up to the eighteenth century, for the Spaniards. Today they cultivate the land and raise cattle. They use llamas as beasts of burden, worship horses, and live in ranchos made of clay or corrugated iron sheets. The village on the left is called San Cristóbal. We got lodgings there. During the first weeks we filmed hummingbirds, butterflies, and parrots. We shot many reels of cockatoos, cypresses, magnolias, little children, laurel trees, withered grandmothers outside the doors of their hovels, sheep shearings, the snowy peaks of the Cordillera in the east. In short, we behaved as if we were filming a school essay entitled "My Most Wonderful Holiday Experience!"

"Expensive school essay," groaned Mr. Drinkwater. "And all of it on *my* money." But then he became as quiet as a mouse. Because on the screen there appeared an old, gray fortress. With battlements and loopholes and a squat round tower. Armed guards patrolled the walls behind the loopholes.

"So that's where Señor Lopez lives," breathed Maxie, excitedly.

"The place is a castle that was built in the seventeenth century by one of the Spanish viceroys," the Inspector informed them. "Successive governor generals resided there during their tours of inspection. There they tried criminal cases, and from there they sent punitive expeditions against rebellious Indians. Later the fortress fell into ruin. Lopez bought it thirty years ago and had the massive walls rebuilt and the most modern equipment installed. His own radio station, his own waterworks, his own electricity. It's all there. What he doesn't have doesn't exist."

"Did you get inside, then?" asked Maxie excitedly.

"Oh, yes. More of that later. What you see now is the rectangular inner courtyard. It's laid out in concrete slabs as far as the rose garden on the left. The girls prancing about in swimsuits are the dancers who entertain the señor every evening. They are practicing."

"Rather old girls," said Rosa Marzipan.

"No wonder," said Inspector Steinbeiss. "Ten years ago they were kidnapped from a nightclub in Mexico City, and they weren't in the first flower of youth even then."

"Take them with the zoom lens?" asked Hokus.

"Yes."

"But where on earth did you stand your camera?" asked Mr. Drinkwater.

"It wasn't standing, it was hanging from the top of a two-hundred-foot-high araucaria, one of the gigantic conifers that grow there. Our Indians had fixed up a high platform. The cameraman was hauled up there when it was dark and brought down again the following night. An airy perch."

"Are those snipers coming into the courtyard?" asked Maxie.

"Yes. Changing of the guard," Inspector Steinbeiss explained.

"The group on the left is coming from lunch, while the group on the right is going to lunch."

"Weary lions," said Hokus disparagingly.

"Weary?" Maxie seemed to doubt it.

"Quiet, please," ordered the Inspector. "The van approaching the gate of the fortress belongs to Miguel, a cattle breeder. He brings them fresh meat three times a week, as well as sausages, fat, and fowls. The Indian squatting under the canvas top is no Indian but Mackintosh, the detective. He has dyed his hair."

"And how was the van photographed?" asked Mr. Drinkwater. "From a second truck?"

"That's right. We were ten yards behind in the truck belonging to Gonzales, delivering fruit and vegetables. Richardson was lying under four banana stalks with his hand camera. He thought his back would break."

"Were you disguised as an Indian too?" asked Maxie.

"Of course. Now watch. The gate's opening."

The gate to the fortress was indeed opening. Miguel's van braked to a stop in the middle of the courtyard. Mackintosh jumped out of the van, raised the canvas hood, and lifted out on his shoulders a slaughtered calf. A few men came trotting up and helped with the unloading. When one of them shouldered half an ox, Maxie cried, "Look! That's Bald Otto!"

"That's right," said Inspector Steinbeiss. "That's him. And the man with the white apron and chef's cap coming into the picture now is the chief cook, Monsieur Gérard, winner of three gold medals. He was married to three women—all, unfortunately, at the same time—so he had no objection when Lopez offered to help him out of the mess. But now I want you to watch very carefully. The camera is panning across to the rose garden. We can see a portly gentleman."

The gentleman was wearing a suit of raw silk and a straw hat and was carefully cutting a dark red rose. On his short, thick fingers rings flashed and sparkled like a jeweler's display window.

"That must be him," breathed Maxie.

"That's the fellow," said the Inspector. "That is Señor Lopez, the richest man in the world. He has people kidnapped. They entertain him and in return are kept in food and drink. They live in a kind of zoo for rare human beings."

Maxie groaned, "And that is where I would have landed!"

Señor Lopez waddled across the courtyard. He stopped beside Miguel's delivery van, spoke to the French chef, and examined, as he sniffed at his rose, the ox half that was being unloaded. Then he nodded, turned, and went across to a building in whose doorway an ancient, filthy-haired crone was waiting for him. The pair disappeared into the house.

"That was the gipsy he has to tell his fortune," the Inspector explained. "And now two Indians carrying a banana stalk are coming into the picture. They are stacking the fruit and vegetables near Miguel's van so that Richardson the cameraman will not be discovered in the second van. One of the Indians is Gonzales, a peasant, and the other is known, in ordinary life, by the name of Steinbeiss."

Mr. Drinkwater laughed. "Unrecognizable!" All the others in the projection room laughed at the Inspector's talent for disguise.

Only Maxie was not altogether happy. "It's a good thing Bernhard didn't see you," he said, his voice shaking. "Because Bernhard would probably have recognized you."

"You're almost as sharp as Bernhard yourself," said Steinbeiss. "A week later, when I went there to unload goods for the third time, that confounded crook did put in an appearance. He had a toothpick between his lips and stood by idly watching us. Suddenly he started, and before I could do anything, put his hand to my face. Brown greasepaint came off on his fingers. Then everything happened very quickly. I let him have it on the jaw. His eyes rolled up and he fell over backwards. Gonzales dropped the bananas. They dropped on Bernhard's breadbasket. Mackintosh and Miguel jumped into the first van, and Gonzales and I into the second, and before the guards realized what was up, we were roaring through the gate. There were a few shots. No one was injured."

"Either they were no snipers," said Hokus, "or they fired into the air."

"They fired into the air. At least, that's what they said after their arrest."

"They were arrested?" asked Rosa Marzipan.

"Along with Señor Lopez?" cried Maxie.

"That's another story," said the Inspector, and his voice sounded very sad. Then he pressed a control button, and the film started again. "The other cameraman was still perched up in his conifer. The pictures you are seeing now were made by him two hours after our flight from the fortress. Pay close attention. You're about to witness my defeat."

They all stared spellbound at the screen. They could see the empty courtyard. But wait—is was not quite empty. Beside the rose bed stood a portly, elegantly dressed man. He was wearing a suit of raw silk and a straw hat and was carefully cutting himself a dark red rose. Then he turned around, sniffing the rose; he seemed to be waiting for something.

"The fellow has nerves of steel," muttered Mr. Drinkwater.

Suddenly the concrete slabs of the courtyard slid apart. A subterranean hanger was revealed. And out of the hangar a jet plane rose slowly. The concrete platform on which it was standing fitted exactly into the space left by the concrete slabs that had slid to one side. Señor Lopez waddled across to the plane. The door opened and a ladder was lowered. Señor

Lopez climbed aboard. The ladder was drawn up; the door closed. Immediately the plane rose vertically in the air and then vanished over the horizon. Then the sky was as empty as the courtyard.

"Vertical take-off jet," Maxie stated.

"Quite correct," growled Herr Steinbeiss. "But such aircraft are still not off the drawing board, at least not for use by the general public."

"Why should the richest man in the world wait for that?" demanded Mr. Drinkwater. "A test pilot loses his bearings. Well? The plane vanishes. The pilot vanishes. So? Maybe it's lying crashed somewhere on a glacier. But maybe the pilot was bribed and landed safely in a fortress."

"That must have been it," said the Inspector. "At any rate, at the same time that Señor Lopez and the plane disappeared, the French chef, the gipsy woman, the ballet girls, our friends Bernhard and Otto, the captain of the guard, an art historian, and one hundred seventy-four framed paintings also disappeared. We were able to count only the hooks on which the paintings had been hanging."

"Does anyone know where the plane flew to?"

"Nobody knows. Paraguay? Bolivia? Peru? Lopez owns mines and quarries, haciendas, fishing fleets, canning factories, chains of hotels and credit banks. Compared with him, Croesus was a beggar. He has vanished. To another fortress? To another continent? He outsmarted me."

"Wait and see," said Mr. Drinkwater. "We'll bide our time. I shall have your film shown in every cinema as a second feature with a suitable commentary linking it with *The Little Man,* the main feature. The expedition was not in vain. Interpol will finally have to intervene in the affair. Señor Lopez hasn't much more time to go round sniffing roses."

"Did you interrogate the guards he left in the lurch?" Hokus asked.

"Mackintosh saw to that. They were furious. He took the tapes back to New York with him. The interviews are being translated now. We also got photographs and movies of the fellows."

"That's great," said Mr. Drinkwater. "We can use them for a documentary article for an illustrated magazine." He slapped the Inspector on the shoulder. "Why are you so dissatisfied with yourself?"

"Why did I talk you into the expedition?" asked Steinbeiss.

"To photograph hummingbirds? To film an old fortress? To wave goodbye to a plane? No, indeed. I wanted a little more than that."

"One always wants a little more," sighed Drinkwater. "And one only succeeds in getting a little less."

Rosa Marzipan was amused. "You are a philosopher."

Mr. Drinkwater stood up. "I'm mainly a cigar smoker. And now I must telephone New York."

Everything has an end. Even November. John F. Drinkwater flew to Genoa, where his yacht *Sleepwell* was waiting for him. Detective Inspector Steinbeiss flew back to Berlin. Stilke's Circus rattled off by rail to its winter quarters. Maxie and Hokus set out on a journey to visit King Bileam. And here begins . . .

Where's Breganzona? · King Bileam's headgear ·
Description of the capital · Judith sews, and Maxie sings ·
A fortnight is only two weeks

So Mr. Drinkwater flew to Genoa. You all know where Genoa is; but anyone who does not know can look it up in a school atlas. Professor Hokus von Pokus, with Maxie in his breast pocket, traveled to Calais, got into a jet called *Dagobert* waiting for them there, and flew to Breganzona. Now you do *not* know where Breganzona is; and you won't find it even if you look for it in your school atlas.

Even in the biggest and thickest atlas it cannot be found. It's no use looking. And even in my twenty-five-volume encyclopaedia it is not listed. Not one word about the place, although even the tiny village of Pichelstein is certainly mentioned. One runs one's head against a blank wall. Only in the most celebrated English work of reference, the *Encyclopaedia Britannica*, do we find a few crumbs of information. The entry reads as follows:

> **BREGANZONA** None of the following details can be vouched for. Situation, size and population unknown. Presumably a city and an island in the Atlantic. Originally artists' colony. Constitutional monarchy since 1912. King Dagobert the Wise (1912–50) of French descent, specialist in the philosophy of the arts. Since 1950, King Bileam the Nice, German descent, artist.
> Exports: toys, pictures, books, picture books, sweets, sausages, gym shoes, balloons, paintboxes, gingerbread and cherry cakes, chewing gum, plasticine, etc.
> Imports: negligible. Tourist traffic: nonexistent. Cover address for exports: Calais, port of, Dock XII B; for letters and parcels: Calais, P.O. Box 97. Literature about Br.: none. Report based on rumors.

The flight lasted exactly two hours. They saw mostly water, occasionally a bit of coastline, and finally nothing but the ocean. No waves, no white foam, only goosepimples of shivering water. And from time to time, traveling east or west, small ships.

94

As the stewardess was serving them with bacon and scrambled eggs on their collapsable tables, Hokus asked, "How often do you make this trip? Every day? Or two or three times a week?"

She stared at him in amazement. "Are you joking? We fly only when we have invited guests. And we have such people not two or three times a week, but at the very most two or three times a year."

"Don't you get any tourists, then?" asked Maxie, fishing up a scrap of bacon from the plate. "No photographers and reporters?"

The stewardess clapped her hands over her chic little cap. "King Bileam forbids it! Such disturbers of the peace are not allowed to enter our country. The last one who attempted it was whipped back to his motorboat by Bileam the Nice himself, singlehanded."

"Worrywippimif?" Maxie said, choking a little.

Hokus told him severely, "Don't speak with your mouth full."

Maxie cleared his throat again, until he was able to speak clearly once more. "I only wanted to know what the King whipped him with."

"With a carpetbeater," the young lady explained. "But don't be afraid, my dear. He doesn't go for his invited guests like that." After these reassuring words she returned to the plane's kitchen and took a tray to the cockpit, so that the pilot and radio engineer would not starve to death.

"It's all right for her to talk," said Maxie softly. "But if I were on my own now, I suppose I should be frightened. Don't you feel the same? An empty plane. Only the crew. And nobody knows where Breganzona lies . . ."

"Have a bit more scrambled egg," Hokus suggested. "It strengthens the nerves."

"No, I'm full. Full of worries, too." The Little Man was already clambering up the Professor, and soon disappeared into his breast pocket. Suddenly he poked his head out again. "Take good care of me."

"Better than I would of myself. Better than BOAC," said Hokus. Then he felt Maxie settling down comfortably in his breast pocket. He smiled to himself, lit a cigarette, and gazed through the circular window at the horizon, where sea and sky said, "How do you do?"

King Bileam the Nice was standing on the landing strip at Breganzona airport. He took his gold watch out of the pocket of his brocade waistcoat and said loudly and clearly, "If they don't come at once, they'll come either later or not at all. There is no fourth possibility."

Beside him stood Judith and Osram, his children. And behind the trio forty classes of schoolchildren formed a lane. They had triangles, mouthorgans, guitars, and fifes. There was an air of expectancy.

The King looked like a smooth-shaven Father Christmas. He had white hair and plump red cheeks and wore a hard black bowler on his head. But he also wore his king's crown. It lay around the crown of the bowler, all flashing gold, supported by the brim, where it had been tacked on by the Queen. Otherwise every time he took his hat off the thing would have fallen on the ground. (I mean the crown, not the Queen.)

"Hat and crown are to me one and indivisible," Bileam the Nice was accustomed to say. "Without my hat I should only be a king, and without my crown I should only be a subject. But I am both, and I shall wear both until the day the crown grows too heavy for me to wear. Then I shall take it off, keep only my hat on my head, and paint pictures once again."

Princess Judith was pulling at his sleeve. "Papa, the plane's coming!"

She was right. The plane *Dagobert* had appeared over the horizon; it became bigger and bigger, made a wide circle, and landed on the airfield with its engines shut off. It was escorted to its stopping place by the airport personnel, and there it came to a halt, quivering. The door opened. The gangway was set in place. The first to appear was the stewardess. Behind her appeared Hokus. He waved.

"Strike up the band!" shouted King Bileam, and the forty classes of schoolchildren began to let rip, fit to raise the roof, if there had been any roof in the vicinity. I don't know whether or not it was very beautiful, but it was certainly very loud. One might say it was really beautifully loud.

The reception was most cordial. The King took off his hat and crown. Judith bobbed a curtsy. Osram bowed deeply. Hokus shook the hands of all three. Maxie waved from his breast pocket and laughed. But no one could hear him laughing. And no one could hear what Bileam and Hokus were saying. In the Kingdom of Breganzona there are only twenty-five children to a class, but when you have forty such classes making music, you have a thousand children making music.

Only when Bileam, appalled, put his hands over his ears, did the musicians stop their noise. Then the King and Hokus repeated exactly what they had said before but had not heard on account of the racket. Hokus lifted Maxie out of his breast pocket and placed him on the King's palm; then they proceeded, amid the rejoicings of a thousand children, to the limousine awaiting them. It was a Rolls Royce, built in 1930. A roomy and comfortable vehicle. Despite his hat and his crown, the King did not have to bow his head as he stepped into his car.

"My wife asks you to excuse her. She could not come," said the King as they drove through the city. "She's making some cocoa and cutting sandwiches. She insists on doing the cooking herself. However, she knows that first we shall be stopping off to see the Sausage God."

"The Sausage God?" Maxie queried. "What on earth is that?" He was sitting on the royal hat brim, leaning back against the golden crown; he felt perfectly at home.

"The Sausage God is a butcher," said Osram. "His shop is famous, and . . ."

"And even more famous are his hot sausages," Judith said appreciatively. "No one else can make them as he does. They just melt in your mouth."

"How do they manage to do that?" asked Maxie. "I know only the kind of sausages that one bites into. They crackle, and one really has to chew them."

The children almost flew at each other. Only when the King turned round and said gently, "Don't argue, children, be nice to each other," were they calm again, and the two men could continue their conversation in peace.

"But why haven't you brought along the love of your life, your pretty Rosa Marzipan?" asked the King.

"She's visiting an old aunt," said the Professor, "and begs to be forgiven for her absence."

"Rosa has no old aunt," cried Maxie.

"Is that so?" asked the King, amused, folding his hands over his stomach.

Hokus winked at him covertly. "It's quite right that she has no old aunt."

Maxie poked his head over the edge of the royal brim and wagged his finger accusingly at the Professor. "You're hiding things from me."

"Right again, son. Though it's only one thing. However . . ."

"Can't you whisper it in my ear?" asked Bileam.

"Only when that little rascal's no longer perched on your hat. Because he has very sharp ears for whatever he's not supposed to hear."

"It's the same thing with my own children," the King admitted. "When I tell them to do something, they're as deaf as a post. But when their mother whispers something into my ear, they pick up every syllable."

"Is it a nice secret?" The Little Man wanted to know.

"Your eyes will grow as big as soup bowls."

"And when shall I make such big eyes?"

"In about two weeks."

Breganzona is a gay city. The people there enjoy themselves more than elsewhere. The shop clerks are friendlier. The curtains at the windows, and even the rainclouds over the roofs, smile upon the streets and squares. Anyone who takes a bus more than ten stops receives a free glass of lemonade from the driver. And none of the city's street lamps are alike. They are as brightly colored and as different as paper lanterns at a garden party.

100

When people go shopping, they don't have to dash from one side of the road to the other like scalded cats to avoid the traffic. Car owners park their cars outside the shopping district, take their roller skates out of their trunks, and skate comfortably from shop to shop.

"Usually we do the same," said King Bileam. "Only when we go to meet our guests do we remain seated in the vehicle of state. Honor to whom honor is due."

Maxie did not care at all about so much honor. "But can't we get out? Just think—you on your rollerskates and me on your crown-hat or hat-crown—it would be a huge joke."

"Perhaps some other time," suggested the King.

"Anyhow, we're already there," Osram stated. "Everybody out."

The Sausage God was a butcher of enormous girth who shook hands vigorously with them all. But he did not trust himself with Maxie. The customers in the little shop took no notice at all of the King and his companions. That was the custom in Breganzona.

Whether he took his family riding on the roller coaster at the fair or had a go on the Test Your Strength machine or bought waterfleas for Judith's aquarium or a new record or an egg beater for Hildegard, the Queen, the common people looked politely away.

Naturally they did occasionally take a peep at him. Especially today, with The Little Man sitting on the royal hat brim. After all, that was something they didn't see every day.

Behind the counter the serving girls and the sausage pans

gleamed and steamed. In front of the counter stood seven round wooden tables, each as tall as a man and scrubbed spotlessly clean. There was no room for chairs. One ate standing up, so the tables were twice as high as elsewhere. Halfway up they had a shelf, where the plates for the children were laid. Six of the tables were laden with plates, little sausages, rolls, and jars of mustard and were surrounded by chattering, chop-licking customers.

The empty table in the middle was adorned with an embroidered pennant bearing the inscription: "The King enjoys his sausages here. Every day between four and five. The Sausage God, Purveyor to His Majesty."

"Now I call that practical," said Hokus. "Every table has two floors." The manager of the establishment, who was serving them himself, beamed broadly. "My own invention," he said proudly. "I've taken out a patent on them as 'Two-story standing and eating tables for big and small.'" Then he stamped off to his meat box to fetch a few more chains of little sausages for the steaming pans.

"Do you call such tables practical?" Maxie asked the Professor. "I call them simply wonderful." Hokus and the King bit reverently into the hot sausages and uttered blissful sighs. Maxie received a morsel from each of them, sighed likewise, and then climbed down one of the table legs to the lower story.

Judith and Osram were just getting their teeth into their sausages. They rolled their eyes with bliss. Maxie had a nibble there too; he burnt his tongue and gasped for cool air.

"Now what do you have to say?" asked Osram.

But Maxie said nothing. He had already scrambled up the table leg and was allowing the King to feed him further morsels upstairs.

"Another couple of hot sausages each!" the King called out.

Shortly after that Judith piped up, "Another couple of couples of hot sausages, please! For the Children's Department!"

The butcher hurried up with another four pairs. And Maxie once more scrambled up and down between the two stories. Only after the twentieth round trip did he give up.

"How did you like them?" asked Judith.

"You were right," Maxie replied. "They just melt in your mouth."

On the drive to the palace King Bileam bought five red tulips. "For my dear wife," he explained.

"So that Mama won't scold him," Osram stated matter-of-factly. Princess Judith smiled and added, "Two tulips because we're late, two tulips because we're full. But why the fifth?"

"To make her happy," the King declared. "And now wipe your mouths. Here's my hanky."

The Queen accepted the first four tulips rather ungraciously, but with the fifth her sulky expression vanished. Inside the fifth tulip stood Maxie. He popped his mophead over the edge of the petals and cried, "The later the visit, the nicer the guests." The Queen was so pleased at this that she consented to take off her kitchen apron.

Judith held Maxie in her hand, and the two royal children ran to their playroom, where only that afternoon they had constructed a knight's castle, a railway, and a blockhouse with trappers and Sioux Indian braves. First they started the electric train. Osram shifted the points. Judith took care of the signals. And Maxie was the engine driver. He was just the right size.

Meanwhile, Bileam, Hildegard, and Hokus were sitting in the palace library. The gentlemen were drinking glasses of wine. The Queen was plying her needle, tacking the golden crown a little more firmly to the brim of her husband's hat. From time to time they could hear the children's cries coming from the playroom.

"The palace isn't very big," said the King, "and it's not really very old. Dagobert, my predecessor, had it put up after he was made king in 1912, and in those days the taste in interior decoration was pretty ghastly."

"But the walls are sound," his wife put in. "The rooms were not so low as they are today, and since we installed oil heating, we have no more peeling wallpaper." She neatly bit off the thread. "There, Bileam, your crown's a bit more secure now. I'll just hang your headgear in the wardrobe." She went out and left the two men alone.

"Is it true that Breganzona was originally an artists' colony?" Hokus asked.

"It was a holiday island for painters, musicians, and writers, nothing more. But the world outside became noisier and noisier, the factory stacks poured out more and more poisonous fumes, the wars became more and more disgusting, and the Golden Calf grew until it became a Giant Ox—so the summer visitors settled down here permanently."

"And your nation was created by artists."

"Let's call it a small nation," said the King. "That's all we are, and all we want to be. We don't want to be in either the atlas or the encyclopaedia. We seek neither fame nor fortune."

"You should be glad that Breganzona is such a tiny place," said Hokus. "Otherwise you'd have a lot of worries."

"Your good health, Professor," said the King, raising his glass of wine. "And now please tell me why Rosa Marzipan did not come with you."

"Well, without letting on to Maxie, I've bought a house, and she's making it ready for us on the quiet. After all, we can't go on living out of suitcases."

"Only too true," growled Bileam. "One likes to know where one is. One doesn't get any younger."

"That includes Maxie too. He too is growing older. He really needs a place he can call his home. And he simply must be given some private tuition. Besides, I want to write my *History of Conjuring, Illusionism and Magic* . . ."

"And marry Miss Marzipan."

"That's easier said than done."

"Why? Doesn't she want to?"

"My dear King Bileam, can I count on your silence?"

"I shall be as the tomb, as a whole graveyard, in fact. What's up?"

"We're anxious about Maxie," Hokus declared worriedly. He's always with me, wherever I go, wherever I am, wherever I sleep. It has always been so, and he knows no different. What would happen if Rosa and I were to marry? If we were to have children? He would think I no longer loved him as much. The poor little chap would be unhappy, and so would I."

"Yes, happy people can sometimes become very unhappy," said King Bileam thoughtfully. "What must it be like for those who are unhappy to start with?"

The children were all having a high old time in the playroom. Maxie soon gave up the job of engine driver. Despite the raised portcullis and the deep water-filled moat, he succeeded in penetrating the castle. In the castle courtyard and on the battlements and balconies lay all the knights, not to mention pages, shield bearers, and servants.

After Sir Maximilian von Pichelstein, that noble knight, had vanquished all opponents, he removed the battered helmet from his head, wiped the sweat from his heroic forehead, and fixed his gaze boldly on the horizon.

"I yearn for fresh deeds of valor!" he cried. "Bring me the next foe, please!"

Prince Osram had an idea. "There's something afoot in the Wild West. The Sioux are besieging the blockhouse. How about it?"

"Who shall be victorious, stranger?"

"The redskins are going to set fire to the palisade. Their torches are already flaring brightly."

"We shall extinguish them."

"What with?" Osram asked in bewilderment. "The wells are empty. The water system is out of action."

"Then we'll put them out with spit," cried Trapper Max, the indomitable paleface.

"That's right!" shouted Osram. "That's the way!"

"You're a couple of filthy little swine," said Judith disgustedly. "Don't you dare go spitting all over the place!"

Maxie glanced at Osram. "Who's this gabby squaw? What's she doing, getting mixed up in men's affairs?"

"Shall I tie her on the back of a mustang and drive them off into the prairie?"

But the rough men of the Wild West suddenly forgot their gruesome plot and stared fascinated at Judith's hands. For the Princess was sewing. She was sewing a golden crown firmly to the brim of a round black hat!

The crown was Judith's tiny gold birthday ring, and the hat was just about the same size, for it belonged to a doll, a finger-length herdsman. Now he was lying hatless and neglected beside Judith's sewing kit. She bit the thread off and said, "There."

"Exactly like Papa's Sunday-go-to-meeting hat," cried Osram.

"For me?" Maxie asked cautiously.

"Perhaps," said Judith. And as she set the crown-hat on his head, he turned up his eyes as if he wanted to see it himself on his own head.

The royals clapped their hands in glee. "It fits like a dream!" cried Judith.

108

And Osram cried, "Just like Papa on the postage stamps!"

And Maxie? He was standing beside Judith's sewing kit and could not see how handsome he looked. "Haven't you a mirror in the place?" he asked testily.

Judith brought her hand-mirror and leaned it against her workbox, so The Little Man was finally able to gaze at himself. He took his time about it; he thought he was wonderful.

He walked up and down, waving to his reflection; he swept his hat off in a low bow and cried, "His Majesty is looking in the pink today! It's no wonder. Hot sausages are the best medicine. Especially for the liver and the spleen. There's no better diet."

Maxie was all worked up. He thought up one absurdity after the other. And the little royals nearly laughed themselves sick.

Bileam wrinkled his forehead. "The row's getting worse and worse. Were we ever so frightfully noisy when we were children? I fear I must put a stop to it. Come along with me, Professor." They left the library, tiptoed along the corridor, and came to a stop outside the playroom. They heard Maxie shouting, "And now, ladies and gentlemen, I shall perform the Ballad of King Bileam. I made it up when I was in the tulip. You may applaud. Applause is the staff of life to any artist. Will you let me go hungry?"

Hokus grinned. Inside the playroom there was loud applause. The king opened the door. Only an inch or two of course. They peeped in and clung to one another in astonishment. Maxie wearing hat and crown!

Judith and Osram were sitting on the floor. Maxie was standing beside the workbox saying, "Your kind attention, please! The band asks to be excused. They have whooping cough and are in the hospital under the care of Dr. Mumps. Everything happens to me. Nevertheless, here-we-go!"

He sketched a few dance steps, pirouetted, flung out his arms, and sang:

> *"King Bileam the Nice, tra-la,*
> *Wears his crown upon his hat, it seems.*
> *Yet wears it not in bed, tra-la,*
> *Because it might disturb his dreams.*
> *King Bileam the Nice,*
> *When he goes to bed he lies*

On thistledown
Without his crown
On pillows fat
Without his hat,
All night
Without them quite.
For—
If he wore
Crown and hat
He couldn't snore
Not anymore.
But every night he must
Sleep the sleep of the just.
So he leaves crown and hat
Upon the floor
Outside the door
Or on his bedside mat.''

Maxie executed a few more dance steps, whirled in another pirouette, doffed his hat, and cried, "That's all, folks. If it wasn't to your taste, your entrance money will be returned to you at the box office."

"It was simply great," cried Judith. "You're a real poet, like John Lennon. You could easily be the fifth Beatle!"

"Sing it once more," Osram begged him. "We'll clap our hands in time to the tune and sing along with you. Put in a few 'yeah-yeahs' this time!"

"So will we," said Bileam, entering the playroom with

Hokus. "Come on, young scamp, a-one, a-two, a- . . ."

The five of them clapped their hands to the rhythm. Maxie bawled out his song. The others joined in, usually with no more than a few 'yeah-yeahs,' but by the time they were singing it for the fourth time, they knew the lyric by heart and danced along the corridor singing at the tops of their voices until they reached the royal wardrobe. There they hung up Maxie's crown-hat next to the King's.

"They look like David and Goliath," said Osram.

"No," replied Maxie. "David and Goliath did not hang in a wardrobe."

"And besides they didn't look like a big hat and a little hat," Judith firmly declared.

Osram scowled: "You've no imagination," he grunted.

"But I'm feeling sleepy," said the King. "Come on, off to bed with us!"

Seven

The fortnight in Breganzona seemed to fly past. Often Bileam the Nice gave his children lessons in civics, and Hokus and Maxie listened. Sometimes they drove into the city. Then Maxie, wearing his own little crown-hat, would sit proudly on the King's big crown-hat brim. Thus, to the delight of the populace, they would stroll and rollerskate along the streets. And if Bileam suddenly pretended to want to go back home to the palace and asked, "But is there anything we have forgotten?" Maxie would always lean quickly over Bileam's big hat brim and whisper, "Hot sausages!"

"That's right!" the King would cry in horror. "I must be losing my memory. How about you, Professor?"

So in the end, before going home they would call at the Sausage God's. It went together with city outings like love and marriage or a horse and carriage.

Toward evening, as they sat in the playroom, Hokus would do magic tricks. He had even brought his conjuring tails with him. Or Maxie and he would perform their star turn, "The Big Thief and The Little Man." They were like a couple of thieving magpies. They even stole the crown from Bileam's hat, despite the fact that it had been so firmly tacked on by the Queen, who couldn't understand how on earth they did it. In the *Breganzona Bulletin* it was even reported that the pair had, on Friday last, stolen the eye out of Judith's sewing needle! But I think that was exaggerating things a bit, and indeed the Press Officer of the Royal State Chancellery wrote a letter to the editor declaring that the eye of the needle had never been missed. The story was mere rumor.

The royals and their staff were also vastly amused by the number entitled "The Ventriloquist and His Doll." In this number, Hokus pretended to be ventriloquizing, and Maxie, sitting on his knee, moved his head, eyes and arms during their patter as if he were a doll secretly worked by Hokus. The performance took place on December fourteenth; despite urgent requests, it was never repeated. For it was time to be packing. High time, indeed. Have you ever tried to pack a conjurer's magic tails into a suitcase? No? Well, it takes at least an hour and a half.

On December fifteenth, early in the morning, the royal family accompanied the Professor and The Little Man to the airport. The parting was such sweet sorrow! They all said, all at once, "See you again soon!" The jet *Dagobert* rose into the heavens. And here begins . . .

Maxie counts Swiss tunnels · The secret is out · Rosa has to be fattened up · At the Villa Glowworm · A television broadcast and many long-distance telephone calls · Fairbanks 3712 · Before her marriage Mrs. Simpson was called Hannchen Pichelsteiner

At Calais they boarded an Air France Caravelle jet and flew to Zürich in the company of many happy French people who were going to Switzerland for the winter sports. It had been snowing in Zürich. Outside the airport Hokus called a taxi.

"Are we staying in Zürich?" Maxie asked.

"No, son," said the Professor.

At the station in Zürich they boarded a very modern train that consisted of only four first-class cars. They took their seats in the restaurant car.

"Outside on the platform there's a notice saying 'Zürich–Milan'. Are we going to Milan?"

"No, son," said the Professor. Then he ordered coffee for himself and orange juice for Maxie.

"Very well," said the waitress, taking a good look at Maxie. "But we haven't any thimbles."

"In an ordinary glass, please, with a straw. The young gentleman will sit on the rim of the glass. But don't fill the glass too full. Otherwise he'll get his feet wet."

"Very well," said the waitress. "Just as the gentlemen wish."

The world was white with snow. The train sped along the edge of Lake Zürich. It rushed past Lake Lucerne. The mountains drew nearer. The track began to climb. There was one tunnel after another. The table lamps were switched on.

After Hokus had read his newspapers, he buried himself in a book entitled *Pertinencious Pointers from a Professional on the Perfection of the Ventriloquist's Art*. Maxie sat on the rim of his glass; he held on to his straw and took little sips of his orange juice and counted the tunnels. "Can you still not tell me your secret?" he insisted.

"No, son."

"Boo! And you say you're a friend of mine? Twenty-six."

"What do you mean, twenty-six?"

"The twenty-sixth . . . oops, one more—the twenty-seventh tunnel."

Fat flakes were snowing down. They could see glaciers and waterfalls transfixed in ice. They puffed uphill. Higher and higher. At one station the name read Göschenen. And then it was dark again.

"Now we're traveling through the St Gotthard tunnel," the Professor explained. "It lasts for at least ten minutes. And when we come out again up there in Airolo the sun will be shining."

"Are you sure?"

"No."

Nevertheless, Hokus was right. Ten minutes later, when they emerged from the blackness of the tunnel, the sheer brilliance of the sunlight forced them to squeeze their eyes tight shut. The sky was a brilliant blue. The passengers beamed, and the train itself seemed to be laughing. For now at last they were going downhill. Down and down. Quicker and quicker. Brightly painted houses rushed past. Washing was fluttering on the balconies, drying in the sun. The stations had Italian-sounding names. Everything had changed. But there were still tunnels.

"Forty-three," said Maxie. "That makes forty-three . . . no, forty-four since Zürich." For they were rattling again through another thirty seconds of darkness.

"Don't lose count," said Hokus, laughing. "Otherwise we shall have to go back to Zürich and start the journey all over again."

"Don't make jokes, or I'll really start losing count." It went dark again. Then again it was daylight. "Forty-five," Maxie stated confidently.

The train was hurtling across the plain. They could see green hedges with red berries. The first cypresses and palms appeared to the left and right of the track. At a large junction they read the name Bellinzona. When the conductor passed through the train calling, "Next stop Lugano. One minute stop!" the Professor put The Little Man in his breast pocket and stood up.

"Is this all there is to your secret?" Maxie asked, disappointedly. "We get out at Lugano? But where's the mystery in that?" Hokus was about to answer, but a few more tunnels intervened, and Maxie was fully occupied with counting.

Then the train came to a halt. Someone outside called, "Lugano! Passengers for Lugano please get off as quickly as possible!" So they hurried up. Everything was happening very quickly. Scarcely had Hokus stepped down on the platform than he was opening his arms, and scarcely had he opened his arms than a pretty blonde young woman fell on his neck. "Careful," he warned her. "Don't squash Maxie!"

The Little Man laughed. "Don't worry. It doesn't bother me."

Outside the station they got into a car, and Miss Marzipan settled herself behind the wheel. "What's this?" asked Maxie, puzzled. "Is this a hired car?"

"No. It belongs to us," Hokus answered. "We each own one third of it. Which third would you like to have?"

But Maxie fell silent. They had flown to Zürich. Why? In order to take the train to Lugano. What for? Because Rosa was waiting on the station platform. Why? In order to get into a car, one third of which belonged to him. What now? Now they were driving through a beautiful town called Lugano, across a pretty square in whose center stood a huge

Christmas tree, then along the shore of a lovely lake, past many fine hotels. Where were they going? At which hotel would they stop?

But they did not stop at any hotel. They drove right across town and began driving up a hill rising above the lake. Past villas and gardens. Through chestnut woods and through villages with churches, graveyards, schools, grocery stores, inns, and filling stations. The streets became narrower. They were no longer paved. The car jumped about like a rabbit. But then, quite unexpectedly, it turned off into a field track and stopped before a white wall. Beside the entrance gate a nameplate had been put up. "Villa Carefree," read Maxie.

Rosa Marzipan unlocked the gate, drove the car over the crackling gravel to the garage, got out again and said, laughing, "Welcome! Welcome home!"

So this was the secret. This was why Rosa had visited an old aunt although she had no aunt at all. This was why they had pulled the wool over The Little Man's eyes. It was to be a surprise, and it certainly was.

Maxie gazed at the beautiful, ochre-washed villa with its green shutters and said, "You could knock me down with a feather." And after they had strolled across the lawns, among the trees and flower beds and to the terrace, from which they could see, far below, Lake Lugano and, on the opposite bank, the Monte Bré and San Salvatore with their funiculas, Maxie said, after a pause: "You could even knock me down without a feather." That was the highest praise he could offer, and it was not the sort of thing he said very often.

Villa Carefree was neither too small nor too big. It had room for the tame doves, Emma and Minna, for the white rabbit, Alba, who lived in the top hat, and even for Winsome Waldemar. Apart from the bedrooms and dressing rooms, there was a living room with tall, wide windows and a kitchen in which one could not only cook and bake, but also, if one so wished, dine in the greatest comfort.

They were hungry. They sat down at the table. Emma and Minna pecked at grain, while Alba nibbled chicory. The three house owners polished off veal chops and golden baked potatoes. Maxie ate at a small table set on the large kitchen table and learned, while they were all enjoying their dinner, everything he still did not know.

He learned that Hokus had bought the villa in the greatest secrecy. While he and Maxie had been in Breganzona, Rosa had furnished the whole empty house with lovely pieces of old furniture and in the process had lost three pounds ten ounces. That makes well over fifty ounces, and Rosa had no intention of carrying on such a drastic slimming-diet.

"Other women are overjoyed if they grow thin," said Hokus to Maxie.

Rosa declared, "But I am not just any other woman."

"I think she's right on that point," said Maxie to Hokus. "Perhaps we should start feeding her up."

The Professor nodded gravely. "That's a good idea."

"With Fuller's Fowl Feed? Or is that only good for hens?"

"Apparently. And it would cost me too much. We'll feed

her up, five times a day, with spaghetti and macaroni. That sort of stuff is cheap in these parts."

"Six times a day," Maxie proposed. "With lots of butter, tomato purée, and meat sauce. Until she's nice and fat."

"But what shall we do if we don't like her like that?" Hokus asked. "What if she gets too big for the trampoline?"

Maxie had an answer for that. "Then we'll have her tattooed and put her on show at all the big fairs."

"Children and the military half price," agreed Hokus. "And you can be the barker."

"You bet!" cried Maxie, rubbing his hands with glee. "Walk up, walk up, ladies and gentlemen! Here we have a great novelty. Shown here for the first time, Tattooed Marzipan, the widow of the Emir Omar."

"Come on in, ladies and gents!" cried Hokus. "Her name is Princess Corpulenta. She will read your hands, as long as they're clean. You are requested not to feed her."

"Wonderful," said Maxic. "That's what we'll do. And with all the money we make with her, we can buy a macaroni farm."

Pretty Rosa Marzipan looked at them aghast. Then she breathed, "You are a couple of the most awful, outrageous men. If only I had stayed in Arabia! It's true that all I got there for breakfast was diluted water and ten blows across the soles of my feet, but you two are much worse than my darling Emir Omar, known as Omar the Horrible."

At that they finally had to burst out laughing. Even Minna and Emma, the chortledoves, chortled with them. Only the white rabbit did not share in their mirth. Rabbits never laugh except sometimes when they're dreaming.

After dinner Rosa washed up. Hokus dried for her. And Maxie, with Judith's crown-hat on his head, sang the Ballad of King Bileam.

When it had grown really dark outside, they went once more through the garden to the terrace and enjoyed the brilliance of the dark. Far below, Lugano glittered and shimmered like a jeweler's shop. A steamer with all its lights on was crossing the black waters of the lake. The Monte Bré, a sharp-pointed little mountain with villas, hotels, and villages, looked like a twinkling Christmas tree.

But the fairy tale heaven above the heads of the three house owners, with its golden, green, blue, and white stars—that age-old, sparkling sky surpassed the world of electric lights, however beautiful it may be.

"Don't think I'm being inquisitive," said Maxie, as he was making himself comfortable in his old matchbox, "but whatever happened to my former dwelling?"

Professor Hokus von Pokus sat up in the wide French bed that now was his, and asked casually, "What dwelling do you mean?"

Maxie replied: "The four-room apartment that Judith and Osram gave me."

"Oh, yes, that's right. Four-room apartment. Who knows where Rosa may have put it."

"She put it nowhere. When we arrived here, Rosa showed

us all the rooms. I'm not blind, after all."

"No, that's something one cannot accuse you of. Perhaps in the flurry of moving she forgot to pack it?"

"You're teasing me, the pair of you," said Maxie peevishly. "She would sooner have forgotten her own name than my humble abode. I know that. And I know something else: you're keeping secrets from me again."

"Of course, that is also possible," said Hokus. "It's usually the case round about Christmas. But as you cannot bear things to be kept from you, I shall tell you straight out what we were going to keep secret until Christmas Eve. Well, it's . . ."

"Stop!" yelled Maxie. "I don't want to hear it. I'm a regular little blockhead."

"You're mistaken," said Hokus. "You're a big blockhead. And now switch off the light, will you? The Herr Professor is tired."

"The little Herr Blockhead is too," murmured Maxie, pressing the switch on the bedside lamp.

On December twenty-fourth after lunch, a station wagon drove through the gates of Villa Carefree. Three men got out and carried boxes and all kinds of equipment into the garden. There, halfway between the terrace and the villa, they began to work on the lawn. It was impossible to see what they were doing.

Besides, Maxie had to decorate the six-foot-high Christmas tree that stood in the living room. He hopped, light as a bird, from branch to branch, carefully fixing the tiny candles and hanging up glass balls, little packets of sweets, and frosty streamers of tinsel. Hokus stood below directing operations like a major general, saying, "The blue ball a little more to the right . . . The third candle on the fourth branch from the bottom isn't straight . . . The chocolate bell more towards the center . . . A little more . . . Now it's too far . . ."

Rosa looked in on their work and remarked, "I wish I could take things as easy as you two. I've a good mind to cut my vacation short and spend Christmas with my two sisters."

She was about to return to the kitchen when Maxie asked, "Can't you stay here? We could make good use of you."

"How?"

"As a marzipan fairy for the Christmas tree."

Arms akimbo, she said indignantly, "You are and ever will be the squeakiest, I mean the cheekiest, young monkey I know."

But Maxie, who was swinging on a crescent moon of silver paper, shouted, "Just you wait until you have kids of your own!"

At that she beat a retreat, muttering, "I think I smell the roast goose burning."

When it was nice and dark, they lit the lights on the tree, set off a few indoor fireworks that hissed and sparked, and sang *Noël, Noël;* then they all kissed one another.

"There are no other presents," explained Hokus. "This villa is a present to us all. It's the best Christmas box of all."

"You cheat," Maxie murmured, as cool as you please. "And where is my four-room apartment? And what were the men doing in the garden all afternoon?"

"Well, now," said Hokus, "it's not the custom to look for Easter eggs in the garden on Christmas Eve, but we might as well take a look." He placed the little imp in his breast pocket. Rosa took two folding chairs, and they wandered out into the garden.

At first the two floodlights on the villa roof showed them the way, but then they came to a dark part. Suddenly, across the lawn, they saw something shimmering, flickering, sparkling, as if thousands of glowworms were holding a Christmas party at their feet. But the radiance came from a small house, scarcely higher than one foot, out of whose windows lights were shining and twinkling.

On the first floor were Maxie's livingroom and bedroom with bath and kitchen. In the basement were a workroom and a playroom and even a gymnasium with a shower. There was also a staircase, of course. It led to the attic, and up there, too, in the steep-pitched roof, were three lighted windows.

Rosa and Hokus sat on the folding chairs; they remained silent but smiled contentedly. And what do you think Maxie said? Absolutely nothing! There are children like that. The happier they are, the more silent they become.

Miss Marzipan and the Professor waited in patience. They sat quite still as Maxie climbed down from Hokus, crept slowly across to the house, and peeped through the windows. He was all eyes.

Finally Hokus cleared his throat. "Would you like to have the key and go inside?"

The Little Man shook his head.

"The key is frightfully small. We might lose it," said Rosa.

Maxie shook his head again, ran suddenly back to the couple, clambered up Hokus, crawled into his breast pocket, and said only one word. "Tomorrow," he said.

Eight

On the first day of the holidays, that is, December 25th, he was as bright and talkative as ever. Hokus took a camelhair rug with him, and as the weather was mild and sunny, he sat on the lawn in front of the Lilliputian houselet. Maxie inspected his property from top to bottom; now and then he would throw open a window and shout, "Here's the high bar from Pichelstein!" Or, "My library's here too!" Or "Is this a real telephone?"

"Of course, son. And if you dial 01, you will hear the voice of a lady not altogether unknown to us."

Maxie dropped into an armchair and dialed the number 01. (You've never seen such a tiny telephone in all your life!) "Who's speaking?" he inquired. "Mademoiselle Rosa? Is that her in person? My name is Maxie Pichelsteiner, house owner. A very good day to you . . . What's the matter? . . . Hurry up? . . . Why? But why should we come in for lunch right away? . . . Whaaaat?" The Little Man looked across at the Professor and hung up. "Do you know what she asked me?" he cried.

"No."

"If we two little monkeys had forgotten that an interesting TV program will be broadcast at three fifteen P.M."

Hokus looked at his watch and jumped up. "How time flies when one has nothing to do! Come on, close the windows and lock the door!"

As they were walking back across the lawn, Maxie again got a fit of the verses. He sang:

"To the work, to the work!
There's a smell of roast goose.
Any child can smell that.
What a treat!
And for sweet
We have TV
For you and me
Yes, we
Two gentlemen will see
On TV
You—and—me!"

That afternoon many millions of children and their parents sat before the television screen and enjoyed a thrilling half-hour show. They saw Pichelstein and the circus, the Professor of Magic with his white rabbit and the two doves, the three Marzipan Sisters on their trampoline. And they also saw—the chief attraction—the tiny boy, only two inches tall, who went to bed in a matchbox. They saw and heard how he learned to read and write from Hokus. They saw how the pair went into a gentlemen's outfitters and bought a tailor's dummy and then how Maxie practiced the art of climbing on Winsome Waldemar. The program ended with the song *The Invisible Right-Hand Man.* The lady announcer then told them that the program would be continued on a Sunday two weeks later.

The children were all excited and chattered away about The Little Man until it was time for bed. Even their parents talked about him for hours; they said that if they hadn't seen the little chap with their own eyes, they could hardly have believed that such a person existed.

Meanwhile, the leading stars of the production were sitting in the living room in their peaceful villa, looking thoughtful. "I think we were fairly good," said Hokus. "But I can't be quite sure just *how* good."

"My take-off for the double somersault was awful," declared Rosa Marzipan despondently. "I looked like a lame duck."

Then the telephone rang, and they received their first congratulations. They came from Jakob Hurtig in Berlin, and he swore by his old school satchel that he, his parents, his relations, the neighbors, and the whole of Kickelhahn Street had never before seen anything so fabulous. "You're a long way off," he shouted from far away, "so I'll be off too, else this conversation will cost too much." And he hung up.

"Pity," said Maxie. "I wanted to tell him about my little house. Do you know what I'm going to call it? Villa Glow-worm! How do you like that?"

As they were saying how much they liked it, the telephone rang again. This time it was the mayor of the village of Pichelstein, cut off now from the outer world by deep snow. They were all enthusiastic and felt immensely honored because their village would now really be world famous, which would also contribute nicely to an increase in their tourist trade.

The next long-distance call came from Breganzona. King Bileam congratulated them all on behalf of all at the palace. It had been marvelous, he said, and then he handed the telephone over to the royal children. Now at last Maxie found an opportunity to describe the Villa Glowworm. Judith and Osram were the best possible listeners to such a description. For they themselves had given Maxie as a royal gift what was now the first floor of his villa, the two rooms with bath and kitchen.

The calls went on coming in. The next came from Mr. Drinkwater, and Hokus called out, "Hullo, there, Johnny. I thought you were asleep!"

"No, I had myself wakened. The telecast was very good. I can be satisfied with you all, and you with me. And so, good night all!"

"But where are you?" cried Hokus.

Then an unknown voice said, "This is the radio operator on the yacht *Sleepwell*. Mr. Drinkwater has already fallen asleep again. We are lying at anchor in the harbor of Alexandria. It was an unforgettable half hour. Please say hello to The Little Man for me. End of transmission."

The last call on this memorable day came from the winter quarters of Stilke's Circus. The ringmaster, Brausewetter, was, it seemed, beside himself with joy. "The only thing that mars my happiness is that I cannot be there to press all three of you to my breast. You were all magnificent. You were sensational. You were . . . "

Maxie dashed from the earpiece to the mouthpiece and

shouted, "Herr Brausewetter, what color gloves do you have on?"

"Golden gloves!" the manager shouted back. "Golden gloves, my golden boy! My wife put a pair under the Christmas tree for me. She has a prophetic turn of mind."

And who do you think telephoned again, two days later? Herr Brausewetter. "Professor, are you alone? Or is Maxie with you?"

"No, he's taking a bath in his own little home. What's up?"

"I have just received a most remarkable telegram from Alaska."

"From Alaska? Isn't that somewhere just round the corner from the North Pole?" Hokus asked.

"It may well be. This is the text of the cable: 'Please convey Professor Hokus urgent request call Fairbanks 3712 matter of life and death. Thanks. Jane Simpson, née Hannchen Pichelsteiner.' Have you jotted down the number?"

"Fairbanks 3712. Jane Simpson."

"Née Pichelsteiner! And Hannchen at that! In the middle of Alaska! Where there are also said to be gold rushes, Eskimos, and sleds drawn by huskies. My good lady says . . ."

"Your good lady may be right," said Hokus, who put down the receiver suddenly; he picked it up again immediately and asked the exchange in Lugano for "Fairbanks 3712."

"Fairbanks 3712," the operator repeated. "Very well, sir. But I think that over there it's midnight now, or yesterday."

"I want a lightning call."

"Very well, Herr Professor. And thank you very much for the splendid TV show yesterday. It was out of this world!"

After lunch Hokus complained of headache; he lay down on the sofa, said he needed quiet, and begged the other two to go for a walk. They had no objection to that. But before they went out Rosa forced him to take two aspirins. He didn't much feel like taking them, for in fact he had no headache at all.

When the pair were out of the house, he sat beside the telephone and waited. He hardly knew himself why he had said not a word about Fairbanks 3712 to the others.

Meanwhile, Rosa and Maxie were driving across to Carona, where there are a tiny old donkey and a bleating old goat to be seen. For years they have been standing gazing over a crumbling old wall at the street while being photographed by tourists. Then they drove on to Morcote and along the shore of Lake Lugano to Melide.

There they gazed with delight at *La Suisse Miniature* or Switzerland in Miniature, a model built in the open air for children, with mountains and castles, lakes and towns, steamers, railways, and omnibuses. There one can comfortably stroll round Switzerland in fifteen minutes. Maxie sat in Rosa's coat pocket. When they were getting back into the car, he said, "That's the land for me! Just my size!"

In Lugano they visited the Kursaal Café, where a charming headwaiter served them hot chocolate and fresh pineapple tarts.

When they got home to the villa, Rosa wanted to give the Professor another two aspirins. But he refused them, saying, "I didn't have a headache. I just wanted to get rid of the pair of you for a while."

"A nice man I've picked for a husband," Rosa said to Maxie.

"A tonorious deceiver," Maxie said to Rosa.

"A notorious deceiver," she corrected him.

"Quiet!" the Professor roared. "I've just been telephoning to Alaska. Speaking to a Mrs. Jane Simpson. She said in her cable to Brausewetter, who called me up this morning, that it was a matter of life and death. What could that mean, I wondered. Her maiden name was Hannchen Pichelsteiner. I immediately booked a call, pretended to have a headache, swallowed two frightful aspirins, and asked you to go out for the afternoon."

Rosa sat on the sofa. Maxie was sitting on the arm of the sofa. Each was silent as the other.

"About an hour ago my connection came through. I talked for a long time with Mrs. Simpson, and she promised me to pack her bags at once. Tomorrow I shall cable her the money for her fare, and if all goes well we shall celebrate New Year's Eve with both of them."

"With both of them?" asked Rosa. "What do you mean, with both of them?"

"Mrs. Simpson has a daughter. Miss Emily Simpson is nine years old, and we might address her, if she agrees, as Emilia. Or Miss Emmy. We'll find something suitable."

Maxie sat as still as a statue.

"They saw us on TV and wept all evening," the Professor continued. "Mrs. Simpson appears to be an unfortunate little lady."

"*How* little?" breathed Maxie.

"One and a half feet tall."

"And why unfortunate?" asked Rosa.

"She didn't like it in Pichelstein. That's how it began. Ten years ago she ran away under cover of darkness. She didn't want to marry a Pichelsteiner. She wanted a proper full-sized man and proper full-sized children three times as big as herself. 'Good morning,' people would say to the children. 'And who is the little old lady holding your hands?' 'Oh, that's our Mom,' the children would answer, smiling with pleasure. That was Hannchen Pichelsteiner's dearest dream. She stowed away on a cargo ship to Canada. The sailor who concealed her was reprimanded by the captain and fired. And because the sailor, whose name was Simpson, was a proper full-sized man, they got married. He found work as a packer in a cannery. Then he was taken on as agent for a fur farm in Alaska. It was there that Mrs. Simpson gave birth to a daughter. And the next day—Mr. Simpson disappeared. He never came back."

"I can't understand that," said Rosa. "Was he very disappointed that the child wasn't a boy? Girls can also be quite nice. Myself, for example . . ."

But she did not finish her sentence, for Maxie was tearing his hair and crying, "My dear, dear Hokus, please, please tell me how big her daughter is! I can't stand it any longer!"

"You've already guessed," said Hokus, smiling.

"Is she really . . ."

"She is really just as little as you are."

And here begins . . .

THE LAST

Friendship at first sight · Milly cooks Tommyrot with toffee sauce ·
Mrs. Simpson wants to leave and stays · What are male buttonholes?
Wedding eve and Ash Wednesday · Maxie and Milly won't tell
what they laughed about

When Mrs. Jane Simpson (from Fairbanks, Alaska) stepped out of the plane at Kloten airport in Zürich and had her passport stamped at the Immigration Desk, no one showed any surprise that she was only a foot and a half tall. People at international airports have long since grown accustomed to seeing extraordinary sights.

Even if someone with two heads or with no head at all were to appear, even then there would not be the least excitement.

As I have said, no one remarked on Mrs. Simpson, only a foot and a half tall in her sealskin coat. Nor did anyone notice that, with a swift and worried gesture, she placed something in Hokus's hand, nor that he transferred that something care-

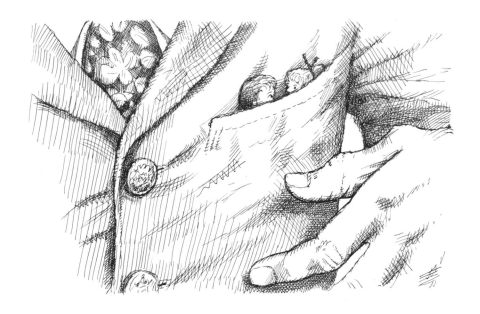

fully to his breast pocket. Only then did they exchange formal greetings. Mrs. Simpson had tears of sheer gratitude in her eyes. Rosa Marzipan cheerfully declared she was overdoing it a bit. And the Professor flagged down a taxi.

So now there are two Hop o' My Thumbs in his breast pocket. "I hope they have enough room," he thought. "I must speak to my tailor about it." Then he twisted his neck, turned down his eyes and tried to squint into his own pocket. He could see Maxie's mophead, and, right next to it, a tiny ponytail hairdo tied with a red velvet ribbon. That was Miss Emily Simpson!

The Little Man and The Little Miss stared at each other without a word, though they were both smiling. Later Maxie felt a little hand stealing into his. He pressed it warmly.

Nine (the Last)

It was friendship at first sight, and no wonder. It's not every day one hits the jackpot, but only once in a lifetime, and even that's not quite certain. Most of us draw blanks all the time, or by the skin of our teeth we manage to make off with a small consolation prize. But we mustn't be envious. Envy turns one's complexion green.

In the train to Lugano they were still very bashful and reserved. Actually, Maxie had wanted to count all the tunnels with her, but he didn't dare open his mouth. He felt as if someone had gagged him with a strip of adhesive tape.

It was not until they had entered the ten-minute-long St. Gotthard Tunnel that he summoned up courage enough to whisper into her ear, "I shall call you Milly."

Then she laughed softly and whispered back, "Maxie and Milly! That sounds very pretty."

"And Milly and Maxie," he added, "sounds even prettier. Moreover, it's more polite."

At that moment the train came out of the tunnel, and the southern sun was full upon them. They blinked their eyes and laughed. "I never dreamed it could be so beautiful," said Milly wonderingly. Happiness was something quite new.

The next evening they celebrated New Year's Eve. The following day they celebrated New Year's Day. And even the weekdays that came after seemed indistinguishable from festive holidays. Of course, Rome was not built in a day. And Milly and Maxie did not spend all their time dancing round the Christmas tree. One of the reasons for that was that The Little Miss easily got dizzy.

When Maxie took her for a few flights round the room on Emma's broad back, she had to go and lie down for a quarter of an hour.

"What a shame," said Maxie. "You'll never make an artiste."

"There have to be spectators, too," Milly pointed out. And I think it is unlikely that anything more telling could have been said on the subject.

But when she was cooking in Villa Glowworm, The Little Miss was quite free from giddiness. She cooked, baked, and roasted for dear life. And whenever she didn't know what to do next, she would use the tiny telephone to telephone her mother, who was over at the villa cooking for the adults.

Maxie liked to sit in the kitchen and watch Milly. Sometimes he would read to her. And sometimes she would deliberately cook something really ridiculous. "Today we have Tommyrot with toffee sauce," they would cry excitedly, or "Gobbledegook with giggly greens," or "Violet Cream with stewcumber mustard-custard," and all that crazy kind of stuff. And what's more, it tasted good!

Once a blackbird insisted on coming in through the kitchen window and eating with them. What a performance! Maxie made Milly go to the telephone while he kept the bird at bay with a meat cleaver. The blackbird chirped away at him. The Little Man shouted, "Leave! Or I'll chop you up into chicken salad!"

But fortunately that was not necessary. In the midst of the battle of words Hokus came running across the lawn as if he wanted to beat the world record for the hundred yards, and the blackbird sought the freedom of the skies. Freedom of the skies? It just flapped on to the nearest tree and went on chirping.

It is really extraordinary: when blackbirds sing, they sing

as sweetly as nightingales. Perhaps even more sweetly and with more expression. But when they're angry, then they just chirp away, chirp, chirp, chirp, like a motorist who gets his paintwork scratched.

When the battling blackbird had finally flown away, Hokus bent down and asked, "What's for lunch?"

"Goose-liver paste with horseradish and yet more horse-radish," Milly announced. "Would you like a taster?" She held a spoonful through the open window.

He tasted it, started coughing, and said, "Hot stuff."

"But good for the health," said Milly. "Horseradish purifies the respiratory tract."

"And yet more horseradish purifies the respiratory tract yet more," declared Maxie. "Besides, it's a jolly sort of meal because it brings tears to one's eyes."

"You should write down your recipes and publish a *Cookery for Kids*," said Hokus. "That would attract a good deal of attention."

"Better not," Milly advised. "Otherwise we'd have all the parents on top of us giving us a proper spanking."

But Maxie was in favor of the cook book. "It'll teach you to read and write, and we'll have lots of fun with it besides. People will be rather surprised at our recipes."

"I'm sure of that," said Hokus. "And now I wish you an enjoyable lunch. Over at the villa we have creamed goulash with dumplings for dinner this evening. When it gets dark, I'll fetch you. So long."

As he tramped across the lawn, he had a crick in his neck.

Nine (the Last)

That's what one gets if one bends so low down for such a long time, admiring other people's kitchens.

After their meal of horseradish and yet more horseradish, so funny it brought tears to the eyes, The Little Miss and The Little Man sat down in the library and drank hot chocolate from their little porcelain cups. With it they had chopped almonds and grated raisins.

"You're a born housekeeper," said Maxie. "But now I want to know, once and for all, how it is you can neither read nor write."

"Who was there to teach me?"

"Your mother."

"But Maxie, she had to work in the shop from dawn to dusk, so in the evenings she was dead tired."

"Was there no one else? No teacher? No kindergarten? No girl in the neighborhood who went to a proper school? When you're such a little slip of a girl? I can't understand it."

Milly looked straight into his eyes and said, "I can explain it to you. But only if you'll swear never to repeat it to a soul."

"I swear it. On Jakob Hurtig's old school satchel. He is my friend, and I can't swear anything stronger than that."

"Well, in Fairbanks absolutely no one knew I existed," Milly whispered conspiratorially. "I haven't even got a birth certificate."

He just sat there and gaped in astonishment at her.

"When I came into the world and my father saw how little I was, he ran away. I don't know where he is or whether he's still alive, and I don't wish to know. A few weeks later my mother took me to Fairbanks, and with the last of her savings she rented a grocery shop. There was a living room behind the shop. She hid me there until the day we came here."

At this, Maxie picked up his porcelain cup and smashed it against the wall. "Nine years in a back shop?" he cried. "That was cruel! She shouldn't have done that! Never!"

Milly knelt down on the floor, gathered up the fragments, and said, "Pity about the pretty cup."

"Pretty cup!" yelled Maxie furiously. "Pity about those nine years, that's what!" But when he saw The Little Miss crawling among the fragments on the carpet, he leaped from his chair, and put his arm round her shoulder. They sat like that for quite a while. Milly sobbed and wept, and this time the tears were not caused by horseradish sauce. The Little Man wiped the tears from her cheeks; then he looked at his hands and said, "My fingers today are really filthy."

"That doesn't matter," she said, already beginning to smile again, just a little.

Maxie's first access of rage was understandable, and it was far from being his last. For weeks he was so angry that he couldn't abide the sight of Milly's mother. And he couldn't say anything. He had sworn solemnly on Jakob Hurtig's old school satchel.

On the other hand . . . Mrs. Simpson was not so bad as the two parents who, because they had nothing to eat, simply sent Hansel and Gretel out into the woods at night! She had worked her fingers to the bone, selling groceries to Eskimos and Indians, to salmon fishers and fur trappers in her little shop, as well as to American airmen and flight mechanics who were stationed nearby. So Mrs. Simpson kept her child secretly locked away for all that time for fear someone might just walk off with her in a package of groceries. It was a pure miracle that Milly, despite those nine lonesome years, was still a normal, healthy child.

In the living room of the Villa Carefree, Rosa Marzipan and Hokus were sitting on the sofa. Mrs. Simpson was sitting opposite them in an armchair, with lowered head, looking like a nursery school child. But when she raised her head, one saw a weary, careworn woman's face.

"Everything I did was wrong," she declared. "I wanted a proper full-grown man and full-grown children. Is that a crime? Or two crimes? Or seventy-seven crimes?"

"No," said Rosa. "All the same . . ."

"I found my full-sized husband. But my little child was only two inches tall. My husband ran away from us in horror. He thought I was bewitched. I was afraid. Afraid for myself, afraid for the baby, afraid of the farm and its arctic foxes, and afraid of the cold. And in the store in Fairbanks I had other worries. What if I were to fall sick? Or if Emily did?" Mrs. Jane Simpson, née Pichelsteiner, lifted her head and gazed sadly at the couple on the sofa. "I'm not a bad woman, but I was not a good mother. Can you keep my daughter here with you?"

"Of course we'll keep her here," said Hokus. "Maxie would kill us if we didn't let Milly stay. But why do you ask?"

Rosa Marzipan leaned forward. "Surely you don't want to . . ."

"Yes, I do. I want to go away from here. I'm superfluous. Even my own child won't miss me."

"You don't really believe that," said Hokus. "A cube can't be a sphere, and a mother can't be superfluous."

"You must stay," said Rosa. "Not just because of Milly, but also because of your wonderful dumplings."

"Besides, someone must look after the big house and the little house while we're away with the circus. After all, we don't want to settle here indefinitely. In short, my dear Mrs. Simpson, you must remain here because we need you, and that's all there is to it!"

This talk had done Milly's mother good. They noticed it after a few days. She was no longer so shy and depressed as at first. She even managed a smile sometimes when the others were laughing, and then, for the first time, one realized how pretty she was.

Then one day Rosa brought Hokus from his study, put her finger to her lips and stopped at the kitchen door. They heard the rattling of dishes, because Mrs. Simpson was washing up. But they heard something else. She was singing!

Then they crept back to the study, and the Professor said, "Well, there we are. We've done it. She's turned the corner."

"And tomorrow I'm taking her to have her hair done,"

Rosa told him. "A new hairdo gives us women new and unsuspected powers."

That very evening, after dinner, Mrs. Simpson said she wanted to show Rosa and Milly something. Thus it was that Hokus and Maxie found themselves alone.

"A good opportunity for a man-to-man chat," said Hokus. Maxie felt flattered. "I'm all ears."

"During the last few days you've been staring at poor Mrs. Simpson in such an utterly unfriendly way that I began to think you wanted to bite her head off." As the youngster remained silent, the Professor went on, "Perhaps you've heard a few details about their life in Fairbanks. About back of shops, for example. And I'm sure you swore never to breathe a word about it to anyone."

Maxie still remained silent.

"Keep your promise and keep your mouth shut," said Hokus. "That's quite all right. But I haven't promised anyone never to breathe a word about anything. So I must speak to you about Milly's mother. You're doing her an injustice."

"I'm not!" shouted Maxie. He was quivering with rage.

"Yes you are," said Hokus. "A few days ago she told us everything. Here in this very room."

"Because she has a bad conscience."

"True. But also because she wants to leave here."

"Leave? Where for?"

"I don't know. Nor does she."

"With Milly?" Maxie had gone very white.

"No," said Hokus. "Alone. She says she is superfluous."

"And why hasn't she . . ."

"Why hasn't she left already? Because I ordered her to stay here."

This brought the serious man-to-man talk to an end, for Miss Marzipan and Mrs. Simpson came back into the room; they sat down looking very pleased with themselves. The youngster looked from one to the other and asked, "Where is Milly?"

Then Mrs. Simpson laid a half-opened matchbox on the table. Inside the box the Little Miss lay, sound asleep.

Or rather, pretending to be asleep. And Maxie pretended to be angry. "This is the end," he raged. "Give a girl

half an inch and she takes the whole matchbox! And what is the hussy wearing? A pair of *my* pajamas! I can tell by the male buttonholes."

"For goodness' sake, what in the world are male button-holes?" asked Hokus.

"Menfolk have their buttonholes on the left and the buttons on the right. But the distinguishing mark of the female sex is that button holes and buttons are always the opposite way round," Maxie rapidly explained. "Therefore she has stolen that pair of pajamas. I'm going to call the police."

Then Milly suddenly sat up. Her eyes were blazing with indignation. "But the matchbox is mine, *and* the mattress, *and* the eiderdown, *and* the pillow, all of which my Mother made specially for me. So there, you . . . you . . . you male buttonhole!" And then—one would hardly have believed it possible—she put her tongue out at him and went, "Bleah!"

Maxie wasn't going to let himself be beaten like that. But Hokus put a hand over his mouth and said, "Tomorrow I'm going to order my tailor to make a jacket with two breast pockets, one on the left and one on the right side, so that at least you two won't be scratching each other's eyes out when we're going somewhere."

"There you are," said the Professor later, as he stretched out luxuriously in bed. "She's not a bad mother at all. She was so happy, her cheeks were bright red."

Maxie, sitting up in his matchbox, nodded. "And once she even laughed right out."

"Probably for the first time in nine years. But you two were really very funny," Hokus went on. "It's extraordinary, but I feel as if that little girl had been living with us for a long time. Yet it was only a few weeks ago that we picked her up at the airport! Rosa can't understand it either."

Suddenly there was a click, and they were lying in darkness. The youngster had switched off the bedside lamp.

"Hey, are you sleepy already?" asked Hokus.

"No."

"Well?"

"I'm *so* happy about Milly that I can't say it with the light on. Not even to you."

For quite a while they lay silent. Outside, the wind howled in the cypresses. It was the south wind, coming from Italy and trying to move north over the Alps, where lay its favorite food; freshly fallen snow.

Hokus thought the youngster had already fallen asleep.

But suddenly Maxie began to talk again. "There's something else. Another conversation in the dark. Are you listening?"

"Fire away."

"I know why you two have not got married."

"Oh?"

"Because of me. You were sorry for me. You thought I would feel too lonely."

"Don't get so melodramatic," Hokus warned, "or I'll switch the light on."

"Please don't!"

Nine (the Last)

"All right then. Don't leave me in the dark when I ask you: why did you think it was because of you that we did not get married?"

"Because it's true," Maxie declared. "You said so yourself: twice when the circus was playing Glasgow, once in London, twice in the palace at Breganzona, and once here, on New Year's Eve."

"Good grief!" said Hokus. "Spying on me is bad enough. But that you should have the gall to confront me with details of the time and place . . ."

"But you talk in your sleep!" cried Maxie. Not another word, but that was enough. There was a long silence after that. In the darkened room at least. Outside the south wind was roaring even more violently than before. The trees were blown about, and they groaned and sighed as if they had pains in their backs. In the distance a train whistled.

Finally Hokus fetched a sigh, as if he too had pains in his back, and said, "From tomorrow I'm going to stuff your ears with cottonwool each night before going to sleep."

Maxie laughed softly. "What for?" he asked. "Since Milly came, I'm no longer alone. Now you can get married with a good conscience! Milly is of the same opinion."

"What do you mean? Have you been talking to her about Rosa and me and everything?"

"I didn't want to. But she wormed it out of me."

"How? Wormed it out of you . . ."

"Well, you see, it happened like this . . . We were having lunch. We had Startingsoup I mean Shootingsoup I mean

Shootingstar soup with Meatier I mean Meteor meat balls. Then I lay down on the sofa for only forty winks and fell sound asleep. Milly was working on a panholder design from Panama."

"Well?" Hokus asked. "Go on!"

"Milly was listening to me as she was crocheting."

"What do you mean, listening to you? I thought you were sound asleep?"

"Dear Hokus, don't be cross with me," Maxie said worriedly. "And please, you mustn't laugh at me. But . . ."

"But what?"

"I'm just the same as you. And I knew no more about my failing than you did. Until Milly remarked on it. I . . . I too talk in my sleep!"

Then Hokus began to laugh till the windowpanes shook. It sounded as though he would never stop. Maxie also started laughing. And they went on laughing together like that until someone opened the door and switched on the light.

It was Rosa Marzipan. She was wearing bright blue pajamas. She had already been asleep and so she demanded rather sharply, "What's all this wild laughter? And in the dark at that? Are you out of your minds?"

"No, we're not," Hokus began. Then he was seized again by a fit of laughter, and Maxie too joined in again and tore his hair with glee.

Miss Marzipan stood at the side of the bed, took the Professor's hand and felt his pulse; then she said as coolly as a hospital nurse, "Don't mind me. Take your time."

150

Nine (the Last)

Everything has an end. Even laughter that seems never-ending. So gradually Rosa learned what the two had been talking about in the dark.

"Well, then," she said gaily, "I'll be able to put my Marzipan in mothballs and become Mrs. Hokuspokus."

"But first of all you must ask me for his hand in marriage," Maxie declared. "Better do it right away, then we've got it over with."

"Now?" she cried. "In my pajamas? Is it proper?"

"Now!" Maxie commanded her.

And Hokus added, "Otherwise you'll always be Miss Marzipan."

Then she suddenly stood up, dropped a deep curtsy before the matchbox on the bedside table, and proclaimed, "Noble and worthy Herr von Pichelsteiner, I implore you, despite the lateness of the hour, to grant me the celebrated hand in marriage of the celebrated pickpocket Hokus von Pokus."

Maxie had climbed out of his matchbox. He bowed deeply to Rosa and said, "Let it be so. I hereby hand you his hand."

"I don't want to seem unreasonable," she went on, "but kindly remember that he has two hands."

"There you are, son," sighed Hokus. "First she only wanted one hand. Now she wants both of them. Before the minute's out she'll be asking for my feet."

"Naturally I also insist on having his feet," said Rosa and made a second curtsy. "As well as his kneecaps, shins and interarticular disca. . . ."

"It sounds as though she wants to sell me to an anatomy

class," cried the Professor, faking great alarm.

Rosa Marzipan curtsied again. "I shall be a good wife to him, and if his thatch should one day become very thin I'll crochet him a new one." Then she curtsied right down to the ground and only rose when Maxie graciously gave her permission to do so.

"You have asked," he declared unctuously, "for his hand. That is enough. From now on everything will go swimmingly. Miss Emily Simpson from Alaska wishes to join with me wholeheartedly in granting permission for this marriage."

"Many thanks, Excellency," Rosa whispered.

"Don't start smiling too soon," Maxie warned her. "Our consent depends on two things."

"I suspected there was something else up his sleeve," sighed Hokus. "Well? What is it? Out with it!"

"You must have a real eve-of-the-wedding party. With blind man's buff and snappers and all that kind of crazy stuff. Well?"

"Agreed. And secondly?"

"The eve-of-the-wedding party shall take place on Shrove Tuesday. Milly has still not experienced either of these celebrations. And if we have both on the same day it will come cheaper. Milly wants to make red paper noses for herself and me. That can be a lot of fun."

"I'm sure of that," said Hokus. "But there's one thing you've forgotten. You're a sharp pair, but don't you remember what day comes after Shrove Tuesday?"

Nine (the Last)

"Why, the next day's Ash Wednesday. So what?"

"Do you want us to get married on such a sad day?" asked Rosa.

"It's a very practical choice of day," Maxie declared. "There are not so many people at the Registry Office."

The eve-of-the-wedding party on Shrove Tuesday was a great success. Not only Maxie and Milly wore red paper noses but also the engaged couple and, last but not least, the marriage witnesses, who had arrived in good time for the ceremony: Mr. John F. Drinkwater and Herr Brausewetter. They had also invited Inspector Steinbeiss, but he had to stay in Berlin to solve a bank robbery. That had to come first.

Because it was Shrove Tuesday, everyone had put on fancy dress. Mrs. Simpson appeared as an Eskimo maiden, Mr. Drinkwater as a Barbary pirate, Rosa Marzipan as a performing white poodle—but the first prize went by general consent to Herr Brausewetter. "Nobody will ever recognize me!" he had announced that afternoon, and he was right. He appeared wearing absolutely no gloves at all!

Then they all shouted, "That cannot possibly be our dear old Brausewetter," and so he won first prize. And as his prize Hokus handed him a pair of iron gauntlets from the days when knights were bold. They made him very happy, for he never owned a pair of iron gloves.

Since it was not just Shrove Tuesday but also the eve of the wedding, there was naturally a great deal of boisterous merriment. Particularly in the jar-smashing contest.

It's not all that easy to hit a pot with a stick when one is blindfolded, and there were many wild swipes and narrow misses. Mr. Drinkwater mistakenly made so narrow a miss that instead of swiping the pot he bashed in Herr Brausewetter's top hat!

Poor old Herr Brausewetter looked a real sight with his

battered top hat over his nose! And it was a full five minutes before they could get it off again.

Maxie cried, "You looked like the Black Prince!"

"As long as it amused you," muttered Brausewetter, rubbing his ears.

Finally there were sausages from Breganzona. King Bileam had sent them twenty boxes. In each box there were six pairs. In the end, despite a lot of hard eating, there were eleven boxes left over.

"We'll keep them for our silver wedding anniversary," Rosa told Hokus.

On Ash Wednesday they all drove down to Lugano together to the Registry Office. Maxie had been right: the town hall was so empty that the Registry clerk was really happy when they arrived.

He examined their papers. The bridal pair and the witnesses wrote their names in the book. Maxie and Milly were allowed to sit on the desk near the inkwell. The clerk made a passionate speech in Italian and shook them all by the hand; then it was all over. Miss Marzipan was Mrs. von Pokus. But otherwise, fortunately, everyone was unchanged.

The wedding breakfast took place at the Ristorante Bianchi. The table was beautifully decorated. It was adorned with so many flowers that Herr Brausewetter ate three flowers with the Café Filet de Paris, thinking they were part of the vegetables. The only person to notice this little misadventure was the headwaiter, who immediately had fresh flowers brought in and put in their place.

That afternoon the adults, exhausted by all the festivities, sat in the livingroom of the Villa Carefree sipping strong black coffee. Mr. Drinkwater gave them a report on the success of the TV series *The Little Man* as well as on the arrangements for the first showings of the movie which were to be held in a thousand cinemas that Easter. And he also mentioned that the documentary on Señor Lopez had attracted great attention. Interpol was hot on his heels.

"He'll buy them off," Herr Brausewetter declared. "He's well-heeled enough." This was no world-shaking witticism, but because he'd made it himself, he laughed until he got a stomach-ache. Or maybe the floral decorations also had something to do with it. Who knows? It is difficult to plumb the depths of any man.

"Now for something more important than your stomach-ache," said Mr. Drinkwater. "I made a plan yesterday."

"Forget it," said Hokus.

"Wait a minute," cried Mr. Drinkwater. "You haven't heard what it is yet."

"Of course I know what it is. You want to make a film with Maxie and Milly."

"You're a mindreader. The movie will be called *The Little Man and The Little Miss.*"

"That sounds nice," said Mrs. Simpson, gazing expectantly at the movie mogul from America.

Mr. Drinkwater began, "First of all I'd like to . . ."

"I feel just the same way," the Professor broke in, "and

Nine (the Last)

I'd like another cup of coffee. What about the ladies of the house marching into the kitchen and making some fresh coffee, one that speaks all languages, even Turkish maybe?"

"Very well, Master," whispered Rosa and gave an oriental bow. Then she winked at the "master" and drew Milly's mother with her into the kitchen.

"What's all this for?" Mr. Drinkwater asked testily. "Why do I have to drink Turkish coffee?"

"So that Mrs. Simpson doesn't hear what I'm going to tell you, straight from the shoulder," Hokus explained, and his voice sounded very masterful. "You are *not* going to make that film! Milly and her mother have scarcely recovered from their awful time in Alaska when you come along and want to send them back, as actresses, to the same wretched place. Are you out of your mind?"

"All in all, he's a good sort," Herr Brausewetter said. "But when it comes to potsmashing or filmmaking, he's like a bull in a china shop."

Mr. Drinkwater chewed his lower lip a while. Then he said, "Okay, gentlemen."

"So you're giving up your plan?" asked Hokus, relieved.

Mr. Drinkwater grinned. "We'll talk about that next year," he said.

Milly and Maxie were sitting comfortably at an open window of their Villa Glowworm, enjoying themselves doing nothing. It was a compulsory subject on their school time-table, which was hanging on the wall: "Doing Nothing, every day from 3 to 4, Sundays included." That is what Hokus had writen in copperplate handwriting.

Maxie glanced at the ticking clock over the sofa. "Another four minutes," he stated. "What shall we play? Betty Birdcage at the Barber's? Or The Opera Singer with the Nasty Cough?"

"Until four o'clock strikes, I'm doing nothing," said Milly, and she gazed at the daisies outside the window. They were as big as Milly herself. And beside them there was a dandelion puffball that was easily a head taller.

"Or shall we try the gymnasium?" he suggested. "I'll do the giant circle on the high bar, and you'll catch me when I land on the mat. How about that? No?"

She put a finger to her lips.

"All right," he muttered. "Lazy, lazier, laziest." And then they stared at the lawn until the clock struck four. "There!" he exclaimed, eager for action. "Let's go! But where?"

Milly laughed at him. "I know what. Let's play The Littlest Married Couple in the World. That's a game just perfect for us because other children are too big for it."

Maxie was raring to go. "Oh, yes!" he shouted. "How shall we begin? With an eve-of-the-wedding party?"

"I should think not!" she said, horrified. "Smashing crockery! Just like you!"

"Or suppose we've already been married one year, and I'm coming home from a journey. We fling our arms round one another, and rejoice to find each other well . . ."

"And then you ask where the children are," said Milly.

Nine (the Last)

"This is such great fun, Maxie."

"What do you mean, children?" Maxie asked.

"Why, our own children!" she retorted. "After all, we're married and have two children. A little boy and a little girl. He's called Fridolin, and she perhaps is called Kunigunde. How about that?"

"Fridolin and Kunigunde? Fine. Let's get going!" He was already racing out of the room. Milly smoothed her skirt and sat down to wait for him on the carpet.

Then she heard heavy steps in the hall and a voice calling, "Hullo! Where is my beloved wife?"

"Here I am, husband dear," she called back. "Your beloved spouse is in here." She opened her arms as wide as she could.

Maxie tore open the door, beamed at her, and said, "I'm back! You look in the pink," he added. Then he stumbled over the edge of the carpet and fell, not in her arms but on his nose. That made them giggle, but that soon passed.

While they were sitting holding hands on the sofa, she asked sweetly, "How's your cough? How was your business? Are you very hungry? How was the plane flight? Is my darling very tired? Shall I get your dressing gown? Why don't you say something, my treasure?"

Maxie stretched luxuriously. "Home at last," he said. "Back in peace within one's own four walls . . ."

She nudged him and whispered, "Now's when you ought to ask about the children."

He gave a brief nod. Then he asked, "Did we not have

159

some children before I set out on my journey? Was it two or three?"

"Two, husband dearest. Golden-haired Fridolin, and Kunigunde our little sugar baby."

"That's right, beloved spouse! Have they grown a good deal since I left?"

"I'm afraid not. I measured them yesterday with the ruler. Fridolin and Kunigunde are still only half an inch tall, as before. That's not very big. Yet they eat like an army on the march."

"Half an inch is one twenty-fourth of a foot."

"True, my clever husband dear."

"And what are they doing now, when they should be crawling all over their father?"

"Don't scold me," Milly begged him. "But I had to take them to the laundromat. I pegged them out to dry there."

Maxie looked horrified. "Tell me what happened or I'll smash the sideboard to bits," he growled.

"I suddenly missed them. I shouted for them and looked and crawled all over the house. Gone. Finally I thought of the vacuum cleaner! I had just vacuumed all the rooms . . . ."

"And the vacuum cleaner had sucked in the children?"

"Yes. They were sitting up to their ears in dirt when I took out the bag. Dust and fluff off the carpet and cigarette ash and garden dirt—and our two little sweetypies in the middle of it all! I could hardly recognize them. Covered with dust and dirt, coughing and sneezing, with red noses, and you should have heard them bawling!"

"Poor little sweetypies," said Maxie, moved.

"I put them in a basket and whizzed off to the laundromat."

"And then hung them out on the line to dry?"

"They were still dripping a little. But in an hour we can go and fetch them. They'll have been dried and ironed by

then. They'll be as good as new, the attendant told me."
When Maxie did not answer, she asked, "Why aren't you
going on playing?"

He pointed to the garden. "We have visitors."

Rosa Marzipan—I beg your pardon—Mrs. von Pokus was
strolling up and down the lawn with her husband. They had
linked arms and seemed utterly contented with each other,
with the world, and with their surroundings.

"What do you bet they soon have a baby?" Milly asked.

"Soon? I don't know about that," said Maxie. "But it
would be nice. Then we could sit in the perambulator and
tickle him when he screams."

"Him?" asked Milly. "Perambulator?"

"The baby boy."

"And what if it's a girl?"

"Then we can tickle her. But it will certainly be a baby
boy, you can depend on that. In fact, I've even thought of a
wonderfully beautiful name for him. As the father is called
Hokus von Pokus, the boy must be called . . ." Maxie rapidly
whispered something into Milly's ear.

"Not so fast. What did you say? Harum von . . . ?"

Then he whispered the beautiful name a second time into
her ear. More slowly and clearly.

This time she understood him completely; she cried
"Harum von Scarum," and laughed and clapped her hands.
Maxie laughed loudly too. And they were still laughing
when Mr. and Mrs. von Pokus peeped inquisitively through
the window.

Nine (the Last)

"You seem to be having a good time," said Hokus. "You're making enough noise to wake the dead."

And Rosa von Pokus asked, "What's the joke?"

But Maxie and Milly cried out as with one voice, "We're not telling!"

THE END

ERICH KÄSTNER, known throughout Europe for his prose and poetry, is the author of numerous books for young people.

He was born in Dresden, Germany. In 1933 with Hitler's rise to power his adult books were banned and burned, and he was later arrested for being a declared pacifist and writing material uncomplimentary to the government. In spite of a hard life, his books are lively and filled with a sense of delight.

The Little Man, Kästner's first book for Knopf about Maxie the tiny Pichelsteiner's marvelous adventures, was the first book to receive the Mildred L. Batchelder Award of the American Library Association for the most outstanding children's book originally published in a foreign language in a foreign country.

THE MILDRED L. BATCHELDER AWARD
FOR · 1968
IS PRESENTED TO · Alfred A. Knopf, Inc.
FOR · The Little Man
BY · Erich Kästner
TRANSLATED BY · James Kirkup
SELECTED AS THE MOST OUTSTANDING OF THOSE BOOKS
ORIGINALLY PUBLISHED IN A FOREIGN LANGUAGE IN A
FOREIGN COUNTRY AND SUBSEQUENTLY PUBLISHED IN
ENGLISH IN THE UNITED STATES OF AMERICA IN THE
YEAR · 1966

AMERICAN LIBRARY ASSOCIATION
CHILDREN'S SERVICES DIVISION